Zane Grey's

THE SPIRIT
OF THE BORDER

Retold for young readers

Illustrated by
EARL SHERWAN

Authorized Edition

WHITMAN PUBLISHING COMPANY
RACINE, WISCONSIN

CONTENTS

Joe and Nell Talked Together

ZANE GREY'S
The Spirit of the Border

CHAPTER ONE

A SLIGHT MISTAKE

"Nell, I'm growing powerful fond of you."

"So you must be, Master Joe, if often telling makes it true."

The girl spoke simply, not roguishly as she usually did. During all the long journey over the mountains she had been gay and bright, but now when they were about to part she showed herself more earnest. It checked his boldness and he gazed out over the wild country before them.

They were at the gateway of the unknown West. Somewhere beyond this rude frontier settlement was to be their future home.

From the high bank where they stood the land sloped and narrowed gradually until it ended in a sharp point which marked the last bit of land between the Allegheny and Monongahela rivers. Here the two swift streams merged to form the broad Ohio.

On the narrow point of land commanding a view of the rivers stood a long, low structure enclosed by a stockade fence. The fort's massive timbers, its square, compact form, and the small dark holes cut into its walls gave it a threatening, impregnable aspect.

Below Nell and Joe, on the bank, were many log cabins. Life and bustle abounded among them. Curly-headed youngsters were playing around a number of canvas-covered wagons near the cabins. Several horses grazed on the short grass, and six oxen munched at hay that had been thrown to them. The smoke of many fires drifted upward; ruddy-faced women stirred the contents of steaming kettles.

One man swung an ax vigorously, and another hammered stakes into the ground, from which to hang a kettle. In front of a large cabin a fur trader was showing his wares to three Indians. Another redskin was carrying a pack of pelts from a canoe drawn up on the river bank.

Joe turned his eyes again to his companion. Her glance swung back to him as he did so, and her eyes softened. Broad of shoulder, lithe and strong as a deer stalker, he was good to look at.

"We have known each other only three weeks," she said suddenly. "Since you joined our wagon train you have won my regard. I cannot say more. You told me you ran away from your Virginia home to seek adventure on the frontier—that you could not, or would not, work at farming. My sister and I must stay with our uncle. He has come to preach the gospel to the Indians; we must share his life and help him all we can. You say you care for me—then give up this adventure-seeking of yours, and come with us."

"I wish I were Jim," was his response.

"Jim?" she echoed blankly. "Who is Jim?"

"My brother," he explained. "He and I are all that are left of our people, as you and Kate are of yours. Jim is a preacher. I—I cared a lot for him."

"Then why did you leave him?"

"I was tired of Williamsburg—and I had a fight with another fellow and hurt him— Oh, I'm not much good, I'm afraid."

"I can't believe that, you know," she said firmly.

"Nell!" He grasped her hand, an eager light in his eyes.

She pulled her hand free and stepped away from him. "Behave yourself, sir," she flung at him, her former roguish air returning. She looked at him from under her long lashes. "Won't you come with Kate and me?"

Before he could answer, a cry from the plain below attracted their attention. They turned and saw another wagon train pulling into the settlement.

"It must be the train Uncle expected," said Nell. "Let's go down."

Without answering, Joe followed her down the path. By a clump of willows near the cabins he suddenly reached forward and took her hand.

"Don't," she whispered. "They'll see." She tried

to release her hand, but in vain; he grasped it more firmly.

She frowned, and her eyes flashed with spirit. She opened her mouth to rebuke him, but he smothered her words in a great bear hug.

Then, as he turned away, with a broad smile on his face, she heard voices near by and flushed furiously. For a moment she watched his tall figure strolling leisurely in the direction of the incoming wagon train, and then she turned and ran to the nearest cabin, that of a fur trader named Wentz.

Mrs. Wentz was seated by the open window which faced the fort. She was a large woman, strong-featured and with a habitually placid expression. Nell glanced furtively at her, to see the shadow of a smile in the gray eyes.

"I saw you and your sweetheart makin' love behind the willows," the older woman said in a matter-of-fact voice. "You don't need to hide to do it. We folks out here like to see the young people sparkin'. Joe is a fine-appearin' chap. Jake, my man, says he'll make a good husband for you and will take to the frontier like a duck to water. You'll be gettin' married out to Fort Henry, I expect?"

"You are—quite wrong," said Nell. "We're not anything—"

She broke off, seeing that denials would be useless. The simple woman had seen the hug and formed her own conclusions. During the few days Nell had been at Fort Pitt she had learned that frontier folk took everything as a matter of course. These people accepted whatever came along as facts not to be questioned. Joe had hugged her—therefore they must be planning to marry!

These thoughts heightened the resentment Nell felt toward the young man. At a loss for words, she stood with her face averted, biting her lip.

"Where is my sister?" she asked presently.

"Kate went to see the wagon train come in. 'Most everyone's out there."

After a moment Nell went back outdoors. A number of canvas-covered wagons were drawn up in front of the cabins. They were dusty, their wheels mud-encrusted. A grizzled frontiersman stood leaning on his gun and talking to three men in travel-stained homespuns. Horses and oxen were being unharnessed and wagons unloaded to the accompaniment of exuberant greetings and animated conversation.

Nell saw her sister standing near her uncle, who was talking with a teamster. Glancing quickly around, she at last spied Joe unloading goods from one of the wagons. Head high and back straight with righteous indignation, she marched up to him.

Hearing her footsteps, the young man turned and glanced at her admiringly. "Good evening, Miss," he said, without the slightest trace of repentance in his calm face.

"Aren't you sorry you—you treated me so?" she

burst out angrily.

The young man dropped a blanket and stared at her. "I don't understand," he said. "I never saw you before."

The quick-tempered Nell felt something snap within her. She had thought she might forgive him, after wringing a contrite apology from him, but this was too much!

Swiftly raising her hand, she slapped him smartly.

The red blood flamed into his face, and as he stepped backward, hand to his cheek, Nell heard a smothered exclamation behind her, and then the joyous barking of a dog.

Nell turned, amazed to see Joe Downs standing beside the wagon, a big white dog leaping upon him. She felt suddenly faint. Bewildered, she looked from Joe to the young man she had just struck—or was that one Joe?

"Jim! So you followed me!" cried the new arrival on the scene, starting forward and flinging his arms about the other man.

"Yes, Joe, and right glad I am to find you," replied the other.

"It's good to see you again! And old Mose too! But what are you aiming to do out here on the frontier? Tell me—what happened after I left?"

Then Joe saw Nell standing near, pale and distressed. He glanced quickly from her to his brother.

"What the deuce—? Nell, this is my brother Jim,

the one I told you about. Jim, this is my friend, Miss Wells."

"I'm happy to meet Miss Wells," said Jim with a smile, "even though she did slap my face for nothing."

"Slapped you? What—" Then the truth dawned on Joe, and he broke into a gale of laughter. "She took you for me! Oh—this is great!"

Nell's face went rosy-red and tears glistened in her eyes, but she managed to get out, "I—I'm sorry, Mr. Downs. I did take you for him. He—he has insulted me." Then she turned and ran back to the cabin.

CHAPTER TWO

JOE DOWNS'S BROTHER

Joe and Jim Downs were singularly alike. Nearly the same size, they were both tall and heavily built, with gray eyes and handsome, clean-cut features.

"Up to your old tricks again?" Jim asked, after Nell had disappeared.

"I'm really fond of her, Jim," Joe protested. "I didn't mean to hurt her feelings— But tell me about yourself: what made you come West?"

"To teach the Indians—and then, you were here."

"You'll never change, will you, Jim? Always making some sacrifice! Now it's your life you'll be giving up. Trying to convert these redskins will be as hopeless as making a good little boy out of your brother. I want to kill Indians, Jim, not preach to them! Well, I'm glad to see you—but I wish you hadn't come. This wild frontier's no place for a preacher."

"I think it is," responded Jim quietly.

"What about Jewett?" Joe asked softly. "Did he die?"

"No, thank heaven. You left him disfigured for life, but at least you are saved from a charge of murder."

"I'm sorry I *didn't* kill him," Joe said grimly. "The sneaking, pale-faced scoundrel! Always playing up to some girl—I hated him."

"I know why you beat him, Joe," said Jim. "Because of Rose—what he did to her. Well, it was partly her fault; she was too fond of admiration. Anyway, it's over now—she has married and settled down—let's forget it all."

"Jim, what do you intend to do, now that you are out here?"

"I met another preacher who said he'd promised to go West with a Mr. Wells, of the Moravian Mission, but wished he could get out of it. It was my chance to see you again—I immediately offered to come in his place, and here I am."

"Yes, you're here, and there's no help for that. Well, we may as well go along with this Moravian preacher and his two pretty nieces. But take a word of advice from me, Jim. Out here every man wears a knife and a tomahawk, and your being a minister won't protect you. Cut out that soft voice and gentle manner, and be more like your brother. I had my lesson the first few days out with the train. Four fights. Now they respect me."

"I won't run, if that's what you mean." Jim laughed. "I know it's a different kind of life out here. If I can find good work to do, and be with you, I'll be happy."

"Old Mose!" Joe exclaimed as the big dog came

nosing around. "Am I glad to see you!"

"Look behind the wagon," smiled Jim.

Doing as he was bid, Joe found two horses tethered side by side, one jet-black, the other iron-gray, both with the clean lines of the thoroughbred animal. The black threw up his fine head and whinnied.

"Lance!" cried Joe. He threw an arm over the arched neck, tears in his eyes.

Finally, with a last affectionate caress, he turned back to his brother.

"Come, Jim, I'll take you to Mr. Wells."

They started across the little square, Mose trotting contentedly at their heels. Halfway to the cabins they met a big, rawboned, black-bearded teamster. He was evidently in an ugly mood, for as he passed them he aimed a vicious kick at the dog.

"Watch out, mister!" Joe cried sharply. "That dog will tear your leg off if you touch him!"

The teamster paused in the act of aiming another kick at Mose. He scowled at the brothers, then turned aside, muttering through his whiskers something that ended with "durn' parson."

Joe's gray eyes lost their warmth and he took a step toward the fellow, but Jim took his brother's arm and gently urged him away. They entered the fur trader's cabin.

An old man with long white hair sat near the door, holding one of Mrs. Wentz's children on his knee. The kindness that shone from his mild blue eyes lightened his deep-lined, serious face. Joe addressed him.

"Mr. Wells, this is my brother James. Jim's a preacher and has come in place of the man you expected from Williamsburg."

The old minister rose and extended his hand, a smile of welcome on his lips.

"Mr. Downs, I'm glad to meet you. Thank God I shall have someone young and strong to go with me into the wilderness and carry on the Lord's work."

"I will help you all I can, sir," Jim answered earnestly.

"Scoffers claim it is folly to try to teach Christianity to these savages, but I know it can be done. But there will be great danger in going among these hostile Indians—I do not conceal that from you."

"I realize that," replied Jim, "but I still want to go. My sympathy is with the red man. He has been driven to make war; he should be helped into other paths."

Joe turned away, leaving the two ministers talking.

"Kate, where's Nell?" Joe asked a girl.

"She's gone on an errand for Mrs. Wentz."

Kate Wells was the opposite of her sister. She moved slowly and easily, quite in contrast to Nell's liveliness. Her brown hair and eyes seemed to fit her quiet personality, while Nell's blond tresses and flashing blue eyes went with her stormy temperament.

"That's my brother Jim talking to your uncle," Joe told her with pride in his voice; then, in a lower tone: "We're going with you."

"Are you really?" Kate gazed at the handsome, earnest face of the young minister. "I'm so glad."

"Your brother looks for all the world like you," whispered Mrs. Wentz.

"He does *look* like you," added Kate with a slow smile.

"Which means you hope that is all," retorted Joe laughingly. "Well, the resemblance ends there, Kate, so put your mind at ease!"

Kate glanced at him curiously. She had felt Joe was wild and reckless but now she was warmly drawn to him by the tender expression she had seen in his eyes when he looked at his brother.

Suddenly the occupants of the cabin heard a low frightened cry from outside, followed by a loud, coarse laugh and a husky voice saying:

"Hold on thar, my purty lass!"

Joe was at the doorstep in two long strides. Nell was struggling in the grasp of the big teamster who had tried to kick Mose. Three men lounging near by were laughing at the scene and a grizzled fron-tiersman was starting forward with a yell.

"Let me go!" cried Nell.

The teamster was pulling her close and bending his bearded face to hers when two brown, sinewy hands circled his thick neck and jerked him backward. His huge, knotty-muscled arms flailed the air. Then he was flung about and Joe's fist smashed into his face. He sagged toward the ground, but Joe grabbed him, lifted him up, and threw him with a crash against the cabin wall. He fell and lay in a senseless heap on the grass.

"What's all this?" demanded a man, hurrying to the scene to stand beside the obviously highly pleased frontiersman.

"It was purty handy, Wentz," responded the latter. "I couldn't 'a' did better myself, and I was comin' for just that. Leffler was tryin' to kiss the lass, and got only what was comin' to him. He's been hossin' around high and mighty ever since the train pulled in."

"Leff's a mean character," agreed the fur trader. He turned to Joe. "He's li'ble to look you up when he comes around," he said warningly.

"Tell him if he doesn't keep out of my way he'll get worse," Joe answered sharply. "Nell," he said to the girl, "I'm sorry I wasn't around sooner."

As they entered the cabin together Nell glanced at him gratefully, her eyes soft. Her anger at him had fled.

"Nell, you haven't spoken to me," Joe said in low tones, his face averted. "Are you still mad with me?"

She turned to him, her cheeks flushed. "I wasn't angry at all," she whispered, and then, eluding his outstretched hand, she ran into the other room.

CHAPTER THREE

SILVERTIP

Joe Downs lounged in the doorway of the cabin, thoughtfully contemplating two quiet figures lying in the shade of a maple tree. One was the Indian with whom Joe had seen his brother Jim talking earnestly for an hour that morning. The red man was slumbering soundly, his head resting upon a many-hued homespun shirt which the young preacher had given him. As Joe watched, the Indian rolled a bit to one side, his head dropping off the improvised pillow.

The other sleeper was a short, stout, white man whom Joe had seen several times before. He was a slow-witted, stupid-looking no-account called Loorey, noticed by the other settlers only when he got in the way or unabashedly begged for food and drink.

As Joe regarded the two sprawling figures, a gleeful glint came into his eye. He saw the possibility for some sport. Glancing quickly around, he went into the cabin and soon emerged, holding a small basket of Indian design which contained several bits of soft, chalky stone of the kind which Indians used for painting their faces.

Looking around again to be sure that he was un-

observed, Joe went up to the short man and gave him
a push, chuckling when he got no response but a
lazy grunt. Then taking the Indian's gaudy shirt,
Joe lifted Loorey enough to slip it around him,
shoving his arms through the sleeves and buttoning
up the front. Next he streaked the round face with
red and white paint. Finally, he deftly extracted the
eagle plume from the Indian's hair and stuck it in
Loorey's own thick shock.

It had all taken but a moment. Grinning, Joe took
the basket back to the cabin, and then went down to
the river.

It was the third time that morning that he had visited the rude wharf where Jeff Lynn, the grizzled old
frontiersman, was making ready for the journey
down the Ohio. Lynn had been employed to guide
the missionary's party to Fort Henry, and when the
brothers told him of their intention to accompany
the travelers he had set about making an additional
raft for them and their horses.

Joe smiled when he saw the dozen logs fastened
together, upon which a rude shack had been erected
for shelter. He noted that the larger raft had been
prepared with some thought for the comfort of the
girls. The floor of the little hut on the deck was
raised so that the waves which broke over the logs
could not reach it. Peeping inside, he saw that some
of the girls' luggage was already aboard.

"When'll we be off?" Joe asked.

"Sunup," was Lynn's brief reply.

"Good," said Joe cheerfully. "I like to be on the go in the early morning."

"After ye see some red devils with feathers in their ha'r slippin' amongst the trees along the bank, and mebbe hear the ping that whistlin' lead makes when she hits, I 'low ye may want to be back here by to-morrer sundown," Lynn remarked pointedly.

"Not me," said Joe with a short laugh.

Joe walked to and fro on the logs, observing how the raft was put together, and took a pull on the long, clumsy steering oar. At length he sat down beside Lynn.

"Ever handle the long rifle?" Lynn asked after a considerable silence.

"Yes."

"Ever shoot anythin'?" the frontiersman continued.

"Squirrels."

"Good practice, shootin' squirrels," Jeff commented. Then, after a silence long enough to let Joe talk if he was so inclined: "Kin ye hit one—say, a hundred yards?"

"Yes," returned Joe, and added in an apologetic tone, "but not every time in the head."

Jeff gazed at him for a moment. Then he brought out a tobacco pouch, tore off a large portion of the weed, thrust it into his mouth, and extended the buckskin bag to Joe.

"Hev a chaw," he invited.

Joe did not know it, but it was the borderman's guarantee of friendliness.

Several minutes passed as Jeff worked his jaws firmly, pausing occasionally to emit an amber stream at a stone several yards away. At last he made a square hit and grunted in satisfaction.

"Brother's goin' to preach out here, ain't he?" He seemed to expect no answer. "Preachin's all right, I 'low," he went on tolerantly, "though I'm kinder doubtful 'bout preachin' to redskins. Still, I've knowed Injuns as was good fellers, so there's no tellin'— What ye aim to go in fer—farmin'?"

"No, I'm afraid I wouldn't make a good farmer," Joe answered. "I want to fish and hunt—and see some Indians."

"Kinder thought so," said Jeff. "Well, where you're goin', lad, seein' Injuns ain't a matter of ch'ice. You'll see 'em, and fight 'em, too. Ever hear o' Simon Girty?"

"The renegade? Yes."

"He's a traitor. Jim and George, his brothers, are a pair o' pizen snakes. Simon Girty's bad enough, but Jim's the wust, allus ready to kill and burn and torture. Simon and his pards, McKee and Elliott, are right now livin' down Fort Henry way, raisin' as much hob fer the settlers as they kin."

"Is Fort Henry near the Indian towns?" Joe asked.

"There's Delawares, Shawnees, and Hurons all

along the Ohio below the fort."

"Where is the Moravian Mission?"

"Lad, the Village of Peace, as the Injuns call it, is right in the midst of that Injun country. About a hundred miles below and cross-country a little from Fort Henry."

"The fort's an important point, then?"

"I just guess," answered Jeff with a grim smile. "It's the last place on the river—only a stockade and a handful o' men. Only men like Colonel Zane and his brother Jack and Wetzel could have kept that place standin' all these bloody years."

"I've heard of Colonel Zane—he was an officer under Lord Dunmore. The hunters here often speak of Jack Zane and Wetzel. Tell me something about them."

"Well, Jack Zane's a hunter and guide. Quiet feller, but a streak o' chain lightnin' when he's riled. Wetzel's a woodsman; don't hang around the settlement 'cept when the Injuns are up. Nobody sees much of him. At home he sets around silent-like, and mebbe next mornin' he'll be gone—won't show up ag'in fer weeks. He warns the settlers when they ought to head fer the fort, and by gum he's allus right; when they go back to their cabins they find nothin' but ashes. Couldn't be any farmin' done out there, wasn't fer Wetzel."

"What does he look like?" Joe asked, fascinated.

"Stands straight as that oak over thar. Shoulders

wider'n most doorways, and light-footed and fast as a deer. And eyes like—well, lad, if ye ever see Wetzel you'll know him to onct."

"I sure hope I will see him," said Joe, his eyes alight. "He must be a great fighter."

"Is he! Lew Wetzel's the heftiest of 'em all, and we've got plenty as kin really fight out here. Lew'd ruther tackle a passel o' redskins than do anythin' else in the world."

The sound of excited voices near the cabins broke in upon the conversation. Looking around, Joe saw several run toward the large cabin and disappear behind it.

With a quick grin, he rose to his feet and ran to the scene of the commotion. A small crowd of men and women, talking and laughing, surrounded the Indian brave and the short, stout man. Joe heard a groan, followed by a deep, guttural voice:

"Paleface big steal. Injun mad—heap mad. Kill paleface."

Elbowing his way into the group, Joe saw the Indian holding poor Loorey with one hand while he poked him with the other. Helpless terror showed through the streaks of paint on the victim's face.

"Silvertip scalp paleface," growled the savage, giving Loorey another poke, this time so hard that the little white man bent over in pain.

Most of the bystanders laughed, but some of the women present murmured in sympathy.

"This didn't work out so funny after all," Joe muttered. He pushed ahead farther, stretched out a long arm, and grasped the Indian's wrist with a force that made him loosen his hold on Loorey immediately.

"I stole the shirt," Joe said. "Joke—fun. If you want to scalp someone, scalp me."

With a quick twist the Indian slipped his arm from Joe's grasp. For a moment he stood straight, staring into Joe's eyes with a venomous hatred.

"Paleface fun no good," he said coldly. "Squaw play." Abruptly, then, he turned and strode away.

"I'm afraid you've made a dangerous enemy," said Jake Wentz to Joe. "An Indian never forgets an insult, and that's how he regarded your joke. Silvertip's a Shawnee chief who's been friendly here because he sells us his pelts."

By this time Jim, Mr. Wells, Jeff Lynn, and the girls had joined the group. They all watched Silvertip get into his canoe and paddle away.

"Bad business," commented Wentz quietly.

"Never did like Silvertip nohow," Jeff said. "He's a crafty redskin, not to be trusted."

Several yards down the swift river, the Indian ceased paddling for a moment, to turn and look back at them silently, his face inscrutable.

"If ye don't hear from that cussed Injun ag'in, Jeff Lynn don't know nothin'," the old frontiersman said calmly.

CHAPTER FOUR

AMBUSHED

As the rafts drifted with the current the voyagers saw the figures of the settlers on the landing-place diminish until they had faded to mere black specks against the green background. At length the dark outline of the fort was all that remained to their regretful gaze. Then that, too, vanished behind the green hill around which the stream made a wide turn.

The Ohio, winding in its course between high, wooded bluffs, rolled on and on into the wilderness. The ever-changing scenery was beautiful to behold. Rugged, gray-faced cliffs on one side contrasted with green-clad hills on the other. Above all hung a still atmosphere of calm loneliness.

All day the rafts drifted steadily and swiftly down the river. Finally the intense blue of the sky began to pale, and low down in the west a few fleecy clouds, golden for an instant, shaded and darkened as the setting sun sank behind the hills. Presently the gray twilight stole down over the hilltops, and the crescent moon peeped above the wooded bluffs.

"Hard and fast she is," sang out Jeff Lynn as he fastened the rope to a tree at the head of a small island. "All off now, and we'll have supper. Thar's a fine spring under that curly birch yonder, and I fetched along a haunch of venison."

They climbed the sandy slope, to find themselves on the summit of an oval island, with a pretty birch-surrounded glade in the middle. Bill, the second raftsman, a stolid, silent man, immediately began chopping up a log of driftwood. Soon a fire was blazing cheerfully. After laying out a few utensils, Jeff Lynn spoke to Joe.

"I'll tell ye right here, lad, good venison kin be sp'iled by bad cuttin' and cookin'. You're slicin' it too thick— See, thar! Now salt it good, and keep it outen the flame; on the red coals is best."

With a sharpened stick, Jeff held thin slices over the fire for a few moments. Then he laid them on some clean chips Bill's ax had provided. The simple meal of meat and bread was keenly relished. When everything had been eaten, Jeff threw a log on the fire, remarking:

"Seein' as we won't be in Injun country fer a while yit, we kin have a fire."

"How far have we come today?" Mr. Wells asked.

" 'Bout thirty-odd mile, I reckon. Not much, but we'll pick up tomorrer. Thar'll be quicker water, and the rafts have to go separate."

After a moment of silence Nell impetuously asked the old frontiersman to tell them a story.

"So ye want a story, little 'un?" Jeff took up a live

coal from the fire and placed it in his pipe.

"Ye see that big curly birch over thar—that 'un as bends kind of sorrowful-like. Seems natural, fer it shades the grave of a sweet and purty lass. This island used to be called George's Island, but it's called that seldom any more. Men say, 'We'll try and make Milly's birch afore sundown,' jest as Bill and me done today.

"Some years back I was comin' up from Fort Henry, and aboard of my slow old scow was this lass named Milly—we never l'arned her other name. She come to me at the fort and tells me her folks has been killed by Injuns and she wanted to git back to Pitt to meet her sweetheart. I was ag'in her comin' along, but when I see tears in her eyes I jest wilted and says to Jim Blair, 'She goes.'

"Wal, somehow Jim Girty got wind of our trip, and he ketched up with us jest below here. It's a bad place, called Shawnee Rock—I'll show it to ye tomorrer. The cussed renegade and his red devils attacked us thar, and we had a fierce fight. Jim Blair, he was killed, and we had a time gittin' away. Milly was shot. She lived fer a couple of days—so patient and sweet thar wasn't a blame' man of us that wouldn't have died to grant her prayer, that she could live long enough to see her sweetheart onct more."

The old frontiersman sat gazing sadly into the fire. At last he sighed.

"But we couldn't do nothin', and we buried her thar under that birch—" His voice trailed off.

Mr. Wells bowed his head and uttered a silent prayer. Jim Downs looked again, as he had many times that day, at Nell's pretty face. The girls cast covert glances at the drooping birch, their eyes glistening in the fire's glow. Joe looked out over the darkening expanse of water, his face cold and rigid.

"I 'low I might have told a more cheerful story," said Jeff, "and I'll do so next time, but I wanted all of ye to know somethin' of the kind of country you're goin' into. The frontier needs settlers, but it's a hard place to stay alive. Jim Girty, with more of his kind, ain't dead yit."

"Why don't someone kill him?" Joe snapped.

"Easier said than done, lad. Jim Girty's as cunnin' and fierce as a redskin. He knows the woods as a crow does, and keeps outer sight 'cept when he's least expected. One thing, though—I heard last trip that Lew Wetzel's on his trail, and if Lew *is* arter him I wouldn't give a pinch o' powder fer the renegade's chances of a long life."

After knocking the ashes from his pipe, Jeff went down to the raft and returned shortly with his blanket. He laid it on the ground and rolled himself in it. Presently from under his coonskin cap came the words:

"Wal, I've turned in, and I advise ye all to do the same."

"Jim Girty's Cunnin' and Fierce."

All acted on the suggestion except Joe and Nell.
For a time they sat close together on the bank, gazing
at the moonlight on the river. Finally her head fell
over on his shoulder and he chuckled as he realized
she had fallen asleep. He lifted her gently and, carrying her to the large raft, put her down by her sleeping sister.

Still wakeful, he wandered over the island until
he found a great mossy stone at one end of it. On this
he climbed and, with the moonlight streaming upon
him, sat engrossed in the mysterious silence of the
woods.

When the first faint rays of red streaked over the
eastern hilltops and the river mist rose from the
water in a vapory cloud, Jeff Lynn rolled out of his
blanket and stretched his long limbs.

"Wal, I'll be durned," he ejaculated, catching
sight of Joe. "Up afore me, and ketched a string o'
fish!"

"What are they?" asked Joe, holding them up.

"Black bass—and that big feller is a lammin' hefty
'un. How'd ye wake up so early?"

"I stayed up all night—saw three deer swim from
the mainland, but nothing else came around."

"Wal, try your hand at cleanin' them fish fer
breakfast," Jeff directed, beginning to busy himself
with preparations for that meal. To himself he
thought, *That boy'll do somethin' out here on the
frontier, sure as I'm a born sinner!*

When breakfast was finished, Jeff transferred the horses to the smaller raft, which he had cut loose from his own, and giving a few directions to Bill, he started downstream with Mr. Wells and the girls.

The rafts remained close together for a while, but as the current quickened and was more skillfully taken advantage of by Jeff, the larger raft gradually widened the gap between the two. Joe and Jim had to spend a large part of their time quieting the horses. Mose retired to the hut, where he dozed and watched by turns. Bill kept his sturdy arms on the steering oar.

About the middle of the afternoon Joe observed that the hills grew steeper and more rugged and the river ran faster. He kept a constant lookout for the wall of rock which marked the point of danger. When the sun had disappeared behind the hills he saw ahead a gray rock protruding from the green foliage. Ponderous, overhanging, it seemed to frown down on the river. This was Shawnee Rock.

Seeing the landmark, Bill pushed his oar amidships and looked ahead for the other raft. Jeff's tall figure could be plainly seen as he labored at the helm. Then the raft disappeared around a bend, just as Nell waved a white scarf back at them.

Bill worked the clumsy craft over toward the right shore, where the current was more rapid. Scanning the river ahead, Joe saw no rapids, only rougher water whirling over some rocks. The channel narrowed and ran close to the right-hand bank. Under a willow-flanked ledge was a sand bar.

"Bad place ahead," said Bill.

"It doesn't look so," replied Joe.

"A raft ain't a boat. I'm afeered fer the hosses—if we hit or drag they may plunge about a bit."

When the raft passed into the head of the bend it struck the rocks several times, but finally gained the channel safely. But, greatly to Bill's surprise, the wide craft suddenly swung around so that the steering oar pointed toward the opposite shore. The water roared a foot deep over the logs.

"Hold hard on the hosses!" yelled Bill. "Somethin's wrong—I never seen a snag here."

The straining mass of logs rolled and heaved and finally pitched loose, but the steering apparatus had gone awry. Bill struggled frantically with the oar. Except that Joe was finding Lance difficult to hold, he would have been enjoying the whole adventure.

Bill, still making strenuous efforts to get in an effective stroke with the oar, failed to see a long length of grapevine floating on the surface. In the excitement none of them heeded the barking of Mose. Nor did they see the grapevine straighten and go taut just as they drifted upon it, but they felt the raft strike and hold upon some submerged object. It creaked and groaned, and foaming water surged between the logs.

Snorting with terror, Jim's mare reared high,

pulled her halter loose, and plunged into the river. Jim still held onto her, at the risk of being pulled overboard.

"Let go!" Joe yelled at him. "She'll drag you in!" He grasped at his brother with his free hand. Lance trembled violently and strained at the rope which his master held in a strong grip.

Crack!

The stinging report of a rifle rang out above the splashing of the water. Bill's grasp on the oar loosened. He fell over it limply, then slipped over the side of the raft and sank into the water.

A puff of white smoke rose above the willows on the bank. Then the branches parted, revealing the forms of several Indian warriors. With a pantherish leap the foremost one sprang from the strip of sand to the raft.

"Hold, Jim—drop that ax!" cried Joe. "We're caught."

"It's that Indian from the fort," gasped Jim.

The stalwart warrior was indeed Silvertip, but not now garbed in the blanket which he had worn at the settlement. His sinewy form stood naked except for a buckskin breechclout. His swarthy face was twisted in an expression of savage scorn. He drew his tomahawk and flashed a dark glance at Joe.

"Paleface steal shirt," he said in his deep voice. "Paleface play—big fool. Silvertip no forget."

CHAPTER FIVE

WIND OF DEATH

Turning to his braves, Silvertip gave a brief command and jumped from the raft. The warriors closed in around the brothers, two of them grasping each by the arms, and the remaining Indian taking care of the horse. The captives were then led ashore, where Silvertip awaited them.

When the horse was clear of the raft the chief seized the grapevine, which was now plainly in sight, and severed it with a blow of his tomahawk. The raft lurched forward and drifted downstream.

Joe stared at the cunning trap which had brought them to this pass. The savages had trimmed a six-inch sapling and anchored it under the water. Weighting the heavy end, they had left the other pointing upstream. To this they had tied the grapevine, and when the drifting raft reached the sapling the Indians concealed in the willows had pulled hard on the vine to make the sapling stick up to catch and hold the raft.

When the brave who had gone back to the raft for the goods joined his companion, the two hurried Joe up the bank after the others. Once upon level ground, Joe saw before him an open forest. On the border of this the Indians stopped long enough to bind the prisoners' wrists with deerhide thongs. Silvertip stood leaning against a tree, seeming to take no notice of the brothers.

When they were securely tied, one of their captors addressed the chief, who at once led the way westward through the forest. The savages followed in single file, with Joe and Jim in the middle of the line. The last Indian led Lance, and Mose trotted reluctantly along behind the horse.

Although Silvertip preserved a dignified silence, his braves were in high glee over their feat and kept up a constant chattering. One Indian, who walked directly behind Joe, continually prodded him with the stock of his rifle, and whenever Joe turned the brawny redskin grinned and grunted, "Ugh!"

Joe noted that this huge savage had a broad face of rather a lighter hue than his companions. He was carrying Bill's pack, which seemed to delight him, especially when his fellows showed an envious curiosity. The big fellow refused to let them touch it.

However, Joe soon was giving all his attention to the course over which he was being taken. He watched the supple figure before him, wondering at the quick step, light as the fall of a leaf, and tried to walk as softly. But he found that where the Indian readily avoided the sticks and brush, he was unable to move without snapping twigs. Now and then he would look up and study the lay of the land ahead, and as he came close to certain rocks and trees he scrutinized them in an attempt to remember their shape and general appearance.

The chief, seeming hardly to deviate from his direct course, kept clear of broken ground, matted thickets, and tangled windfalls. Joe got a glimpse of dark ravines and heard the music of tumbling waters; he saw gray cliffs grown over with vines and full of holes and crevices; steep ridges, covered with dense patches of briar and hazel, rose in the way. Yet the Shawnee always found an easy path.

Soon after the sun went down behind the foliage in the west, a purple shade settled on the forest and night brought the party to a halt.

The Indians selected a sheltered spot in the lee of a knoll, at the base of which ran a little brook. Here in this enclosed space were the remains of a campfire. Evidently the Indians had halted there earlier the same day, for the logs still smoldered. While one brave fanned the embers, another took from a neighboring branch a haunch of deer meat. A blaze was soon coaxed from the dull coals, more fuel was added, and presently a cheerful fire shone on the circle of dusky forms.

Joe refused to feel downcast by their fate. Almost, it seemed, he was glad of this chance to watch the Indians and listen to them. He had been kept apart from Jim, and Joe thought that their captors treated his brother with a contempt which they did not show him.

Jim sat with drooping head and sad face, evidently sorely disheartened. When he had eaten the slice of venison given him, he lay down with his back to the fire.

Silvertip remained silent, steadily regarding the fire with his somber eyes. At length, glancing at the big Indian, he motioned toward the prisoners, and with a single word lay down on the leaves.

Now the big brave set about opening Bill's pack. The others showed keen curiosity, crowding around and gabbling. Time and again, the huge fellow placed a broad hand on the shoulder of one or another and pushed him violently backward.

Finally the pack was opened. It contained a few articles of wearing apparel, a pair of boots, a pipe, and a pouchful of tobacco. The big Indian kept the pipe and the pouch, grunting with satisfaction, and threw the boots and clothes to the others. Immediately there was a scramble.

One brave, after a brief struggle with another, got posession of both boots. He strutted around in them a few moments, but his pride soon changed to disgust. Sitting down, he pulled one off, but try as he would he could not remove the other. He hesitated a moment, aware of the amusement of his comrades, and then held up his foot to the nearest one.

This chanced to be the big Indian, who with a

broad grin took hold of the boot with both hands and dragged the luckless brave around and around the fire. Suddenly he gave a jerk, the boot came off, and he slipped and fell down the bank almost into the creek. The rest of them howled with laughter and, getting up with a growl, the big brave threw the boot into the fire.

After that the braves quieted down and soon fell asleep, leaving only the big fellow as guard. Seeing Joe watch him puff at his new pipe, he grinned.

"Paleface—tobac'—heap good," he said.

Then, since Joe showed no signs of following the example set by his brother, who was fast asleep, he pointed to the recumbent figures.

"Paleface sleep," he advised. "Injun wigwams near setting sun."

On the following morning Joe was awakened by the pain in his legs, which had been bound all night. He was glad when the bonds were cut and the party resumed its westward march.

The Indians did not hurry, but neither did they use any particular caution, selecting the most open paths through the forest. About noon the leader stopped to drink from a spring. His braves followed suit, and the prisoners were then permitted to quench their thirst.

When they were about to start again the single note of a bird far away in the woods sounded clearly on the quiet air. Exclamations came from the braves, who then froze in their tracks and listened tensely. Presently the musical note came once more. Joe turned, half expecting to see in some near-by tree the bird which had caused this strange reaction in his captors. As he did so the same call came from close at hand, now louder, but identical with the one that had deceived him. It was an answering call, given by Silvertip.

Soon dark figures could be seen against the patches of green thicket. They came nearer and nearer, and then entered the open glade where Silvertip stood with his little band.

Joe counted twelve, noting that they differed from his captors. He had time to see that this difference consisted in the headdress and in the color and quantity of paint on their bodies before his gaze was attracted to the foremost figures.

The first was that of a tall and very stately chief, toward whom Silvertip was advancing with every show of respect. In this Indian's commanding stature, in his stern and powerful reddish-bronze face, Joe read the characteristics of a great chieftain.

The second figure was equally striking. Despite the gaudy ornaments, the paint, the fringed and beaded buckskin leggings, he would have been known anywhere as a white man. His skin was burned to a deep bronze, but it lacked the coppery tinge of the Indian. His forehead was narrow and sloped backward from the brow. His close-set yellowish-brown eyes had a peculiar shifting movement. His mouth was set in a thin, cruel line beneath a long, hooked nose.

"Who're you, and where you goin'?" he asked gruffly of Jim.

"My name is Downs. I am a preacher, and was on my way to the Moravian Mission to preach to the Indians. You are a white man—will you help us?"

"So you're one of 'em?" the other sneered. "Yes, I'll do suthin' fer you when I git back from this hunt —I'll cut your heart out, chop it up, and feed it to the buzzards." He concluded by striking Jim a sharp blow on the side of the head.

Joe went deathly white and his eyes, as they met those of the renegade, took on a steely glow.

"You a preacher?" asked the man, stepping toward Joe.

Joe did not reply, regarding the other steadily.

"Ever see me afore? Ever hear o' Jim Girty?" came the boastful query.

"Before you spoke I knew you were Girty," Joe answered quietly.

"How'd you know me?" growled Girty.

"I figured there was only one so-called white man in these woods coward enough to hit a man whose hands are tied."

"Boy, you're too free with your tongue—I'll shet off your wind."

Girty's hand was raised, but it never reached Joe's

neck. An hour earlier the big Indian had cut Joe's bonds, though he still retained the thong left attached to his captive's left wrist. When the renegade reached toward him Joe's right hand knocked up the arm and then grasped the hooked nose with all the powerful grip of his strong fingers.

Girty cursed and writhed with pain, but could not free himself from that viselike clutch. He drew his tomahawk and aimed a vicious blow at Joe, but Silvertip intervened to deflect its aim. Still, the weapon caught the young man a painful glancing blow, laying some skin open and causing blood to flow.

The renegade was frantic with fury and tried to get at Joe, but Silvertip remained in front of his captive until some of the braves led Girty into the forest, where the tall chieftain had already disappeared.

The nose-pulling incident evidently pleased the Shawnees highly. They jabbered among themselves and nodded approvingly at Joe, until a few words from Silvertip produced a sudden change. They fell silent and picked up their weapons. The big Indian retied Joe and then all crowded around Silvertip, glancing keenly on every side.

"Did you hear what Silvertip said?" whispered Jim.

"It sounded like French," Joe replied, unbelief in his tone.

"It was French—'*Le Vent de la Mort.*'"

"That was it! What does it mean?"

"The Wind of Death."

"The Wind of Death?—What do you figure that is?"

"No doubt some kind of Indian omen."

The hurried consultation over, Silvertip tied Lance and Mose to a tree and once more led the way. This time he avoided the open forest, keeping on low ground. For a long time he traveled in the bed of a brook, wading where the water was shallow, and otherwise stepping where there was the least possibility of leaving footprints. Not a word was spoken by anyone. At certain places the Indian in front of the captives turned and pointed out where they were to step.

Silvertip hurried them over the stony places, went more slowly through the water, and picked his way carefully over what soft ground they had to cross. At times he stopped, remaining motionless for many seconds.

This vigilance continued all the afternoon. The sun sank; twilight came, and soon black night enveloped the forest. The Indians halted, but made no fire. They sat close together on a stony ridge, silent and watchful.

Joe pondered over their behavior as he lay on the hard ground, nearly exhausted. He was suffering from his throbbing wound and some of his courage seemed to be ebbing away. But he finally went to sleep.

In the dull gray light of early morning the Indians once more took up the march toward the west. They marched all that day, stopping only at dusk to rest and eat. Silvertip and another Indian stood watch.

Some time before morning Joe awoke suddenly. A pale crescent moon shone dimly through the murky clouds. Absolute silence prevailed.

Joe saw the Indian guard leaning against a tree, asleep. Silvertip was not in sight. Joe raised his head and looked around for him. There were only four Indians left, three on the ground and the one against the tree.

He saw something shining on the ground near the tree. Looking more closely, he saw that it was an eagle plume Silvertip had worn in his headdress. Joe made some slight noise that awakened the guard. He did not move, but his eyes swept rapidly over the scene; he too noticed Silvertip's absence.

Then from out of the depths of the woods came a swelling sigh, like the moan of the night wind. It rose and died away. The Indian stiffened and stood waiting, listening.

From far back in the forest deeps came that same low moaning: *"Um-m-mm-woo-o-o-o!"*

It rose from a faint murmur and swelled to a deep moan, soft but clear, and ended in a spine-tingling wail.

A cold sweat broke out on Joe's skin and a clammy hand seemed to clutch at his heart. The Indian sentinel stood as if paralyzed for an instant, and then, swiftly and noiselessly, he was gone into the forest.

Once more the moaning cry rose and swelled mournfully on the still night air. It was close at hand!

"The Wind of Death," Joe whispered to himself in awe. Shaken and unnerved by the events of the past two days and dazed from his wound, his strength left him and he lost consciousness.

CHAPTER SIX

"DEATHWIND DIES AT DAWN!"

One evening, several days previous to the capture of the brothers, a solitary hunter stopped before a deserted log cabin on the bank of a stream fifty miles or more inland from the Ohio River. A fine, drizzling rain had set in and a rising wind promised a stormy night.

Moving cautiously, the hunter stooped his tall figure and entered the cabin. It was pitch-dark inside but he readily found the ladder leading to the loft, ascended it, and lay down to sleep.

During the night a noise awakened him. For a moment he heard nothing but the fall of the rain. Then came the hum of voices, followed by the soft tread of moccasined feet.

The hunter lay perfectly quiet. If the Indians had flint and steel to strike a light he was almost certain to be discovered. Listening to their low conversation, he identified the language as Delaware.

A moment later he heard the rustling of leaves and twigs, then a metallic click. The noise was repeated, followed by a hissing sound which he knew to be powder burning on a piece of dry wood. Soon rays of light filtered through the cracks of the loft floor.

Placing his eye to one of these cracks, the man counted eleven Indians—all young braves, with the exception of the chief. They had with them several haunches of venison, together with packs of hides. Some of them busied themselves drying their weapons, others sat down listlessly, and two worked over the smoldering fire. The damp leaves and twigs burned feebly.

Presently the stalwart chief heard, or saw, a drop of water fall from the loft. His gaze went immediately over the rest of the cabin's interior, his expression plainly distrustful. He searched the clay floor, but hardly could have discovered anything there, for the hunter's tracks had been obliterated by the footprints of the Indians.

Suddenly the chief walked to the ladder and ran his hand along one of the rungs. He uttered an exclamation which brought ten eager braves to his side. He extended his open palm—it was smeared with wet clay like that under his feet. The braves clutched at their weapons and grunted.

Seeing he was discovered, the hunter drew his tomahawk, stepped noiselessly to the hole in the loft, and leaped down into the midst of the astounded Indians. His long arm made a wide sweep with the weapon and the young braves scattered like sheep.

Then he dashed for the door but he slipped on the

wet clay and fell headlong. With loud yells the band fell upon him. There was a jerking, heaving motion of the struggling mass, one shriek of agony, and then hoarse commands. Three of the braves ran to their packs to get cords of buckskin. The others held the hunter while his hands and feet were tied. Then they threw him into a corner of the cabin.

Two of the braves had been hurt in the struggle. One had a badly wrenched shoulder, the other a broken arm.

The loft was searched. When it was found to be empty the excitement died away and the braves settled down for the night.

When daylight came the wind had changed and the storm had passed. The sky was cloudless. A sleepy Indian who had acted as guard stretched and yawned. Looking for the prisoner, he saw him sitting up in the corner. One arm was free and the other nearly so.

The young brave awakened the chief and pointed at the hunter. The chief glanced at his prisoner, then looked more closely and sprang to his feet, a drawn tomahawk in his hand. A short, shrill yell issued from his lips.

At noonday the Indian party entered the fields of corn which marked the outskirts of the Delaware encampment.

"*Kol-loo-kol-loo-kol-loo.*"

Scarcely had the echoes of the long signal died away when from the village came answering shouts.

Beyond the aisles of waving corn the captured hunter saw the home of the red men. A grassy plain dotted with chestnut trees held long lines of lodges. Many-hued blankets hung fluttering in the sun. Curling columns of blue smoke rose lazily.

The loud whoops changed the quiet camp into a scene of colorful action. Children ran from the wigwams, braves and maidens dashed out, squaws waddled forth, chattering, and older warriors emerged more slowly in their dignity. French fur traders stared curiously from their lodges, and renegades hurriedly left their blankets.

The hunter preserved a quiet calm, even though when the Indians surrounded him, one prolonged, furious yell rent the air. There followed an alarming show of fierce delight. The young braves yipped, the maidens screamed, the old squaws screeched, and the warriors added their deep war cry.

The hunter had often heard the name which the Indians called him. He had been there before, a prisoner; he had run the gantlet; he had been bound to a stake in front of the lodge where his captors now led him. He knew the chief, Wingenund, sachem of the Delawares. Since that time, five years ago, when Wingenund had tortured him, they had been bitter enemies.

"Atelang! Atelang! Atelang!" rang out the strange

Indian name as the hunter was recognized.

The Frenchmen ran along with the procession, their faces expressive of as much excitement as the Indians' as they cried in their native tongue:

"Le Vent de la Mort! Le Vent de la Mort!"

The hunter saw the lofty chieftain standing with his principal men. There were the crafty Pipe and his savage comrade, Half King; there was Shingiss, who wore the scar of the hunter's bullet on his forehead; there were Kotoxen, the Lynx, and Misseppa, the Source, and Winstonah, the War Cloud, all renowned chiefs.

Three renegades completed the circle. Simon Girty, the so-called White Indian, turned his keen face expectantly. Elliott, the wiry, spiderlike little Tory deserter from Fort Pitt, shifted his gaze uneasily as the hunter approached. Jim Girty, gaunt and gaudily arrayed, glared his venomous hatred for the captive.

Before them stood now the man who merited the respect that shone in the great chief's glance. Like a mountain ash he was, straight and strong, his broad shoulders tapering to slim waist. Thick neck, deep chest, powerful arms showed unusual muscular development.

His face was white and cold, his square jaw set; coal-black eyes glittered. His dark hair, matted and tangled, fell below his shoulders.

Wingenund stood facing his foe for a long

moment. Then over the crowd and through the valley rolled his deep voice:

"Deathwind dies at dawn!"

The hunter was tied to a tree. Children ran by him fearfully; braves gazed long at the great foe of their race; warriors passed him in gloomy silence. Only one person stopped before him. Jim Girty, his yellowish eyes lighted with a tigerish glare, curled his lips in a snarl.

"You'll soon be feed fer the buzzards," he croaked. "D' ye hear, scalp hunter? Feed fer buzzards!" He spat in the hunter's face.

Jim Girty read his answer in the hunter's smoldering gaze. A chill crept over him for an instant; then he shrugged it off and spat again on the prisoner.

The maidens of the tribe walked past the hunter, averting their eyes when near him, but stealing sidelong glances that showed their interest and, in some cases, sympathy. One of them, in particular, the hunter noticed.

She was a young girl of delicate beauty. Her costume, fringed, beaded, and decorated with intricate designs, showed her rank. She was Wingenund's daughter. The hunter had seen her when she was a child, and now he recognized her—Aola, Whispering Winds Among the Leaves.

She passed him often that afternoon. At sunset, as the braves untied him and led him away, the intense gaze of her eyes was upon him.

"You'll Be Feed fer Buzzards," Croaked Girty

That night, as he lay securely bound in the corner of a lodge, he strained at his thongs. His great muscles expanded again and again as he strove to loosen the wet buckskin.

His valiant efforts were to no avail. The dark hours slowly passed. Finally a dim grayness pervaded the lodge. Dawn was close at hand—his hour was near.

Suddenly he heard a faint sound. It came from the other side of the lodge. There it was again—a slight tearing sound. Someone was slitting open the wall of the lodge.

The hunter rolled over and over until he lay against the skins. In the dim light he saw a bright blade moving upward through the deerhide. Then a long knife came into the opening, a small brown hand grasping the hilt. Another little hand followed, felt of the wall and floor, and reached out gropingly.

The hunter rolled again so that his back was against the wall and his wrists were in front of the opening. He felt the little hand on his arm; then it slipped down to his wrists. The pressure of his bonds relaxed, then his arms were free. He turned to find the long-bladed knife on the ground. The hands had disappeared.

He rose, unbound, armed, desperate. Soon an Indian warrior lay upon the ground in his death throes, and a vague form melted into the gray morning mist.

CHAPTER SEVEN

FORT HENRY

Joe Downs came to his senses slowly, only gradually realizing his actual position. He was a prisoner, lying helpless among his sleeping captors. Silvertip and the guard had fled into the woods, terrified by the moan which they thought had signaled their approaching death.

The chirp of a bird broke the stillness. Night had given way to morning. Joe raised his head. As he did so, he saw a bush move. Then a shadow seemed to sink into the ground.

Moments passed—to Joe as long as hours. He saw a tall fern waver and tremble. Other ferns moved. That wavering line came straight toward him. It marked the course of a creeping thing.

Joe's lips opened but no sound emerged. Twenty feet away the ferns parted to disclose brawny shoulders; then a tall, powerful man stood up. He stepped lightly across the little glade and to the young man's side.

"Wetzel?" Joe's lips formed the word soundlessly. The man nodded, leaning quickly to cut his bonds

57

with a long knife. Joe sat up as the deliverer glided to his brother's sleeping figure.

Just as the knife flashed again, freeing Jim, one of the Indians stirred. Immediately Wetzel was on him, a powerful hand gripping his throat, but the low scuffle awoke the other two red men, who leaped up with startled yells, drawing their tomahawks.

As Joe leaped upon the back of one of them, he saw Wetzel's long blade slide into the breast of the Indian whose throat he gripped; then, cat-quick, the borderman wheeled, knife ready, to face the charge of the remaining redskin.

Joe, having surprised his foe, was able to get an iron grip on the wrist that held the tomahawk, and with a savage twist made the Indian drop the weapon with a yelp of pain. Then swinging him around, Joe smashed him twice with trip-hammer rights to the jaw, and the Indian fell to the ground, unconscious.

He turned to see Wetzel and the giant Indian of Silvertip's party locked in mortal combat. Their bodies were pressed so close together that the redskin could not bring his tomahawk into play effectively, but just as Joe moved in, holding the weapon which he had twisted from his own foe's grasp, the borderman freed his right arm long enough to draw it back and plunge the blade deep into the huge fellow's belly. With a groan he collapsed to the earth, kicked weakly, then lay quiet.

Jim stood, white-faced, looking by turns at his

brother and their savior. Joe had eyes only for Wetzel.

"Brothers, I reckon?" Wetzel asked, looking curiously at Jim.

"Yes—we're brothers. But who are you?"

"It's Wetzel, the hunter, Jim!" Joe cried. "He has saved our lives." He spoke to the borderman: "Jeff Lynn said I'd know you if I ever saw you."

"What happened to Jeff?" inquired Wetzel.

"Jeff was on the first raft, and for all we know he's safe at Fort Henry by this time. Our steersman was shot when we were captured."

"Did the Shawnee have somethin' ag'in' you boys?"

"Why, yes—I played a joke on him, took his shirt and put it on another fellow."

"Bad as kickin' him," commented the hunter.

"How did you find us?" Joe asked eagerly.

"Run acrost yer trail two days back," said Wetzel, eyeing the Indian whom Joe had knocked out and who now showed signs of slowly returning consciousness.

"Did you see anything of another band of Indians? A tall chief and Jim Girty were among them."

"They been arter me three days. Big chief is Wingenund. I seen you pull Girty's nose. Arter the Delawares went I turned loose yer dog and horse and lit out on yer trail."

"Where are the Delawares now?"

"Reckon they're nosin' my back trail. We'll have to be gittin'—Silvertip'll soon hev a lot o' Injuns here."

So saying, he stepped to the side of the now stirring Indian, his knife held ready for a thrust. Jim Downs stepped forward.

"No!" he cried. "You can't kill a helpless man!"

Wetzel studied him puzzledly for an instant. "You're new on the frontier, all right," he said. "If I let this Injun live, it may be for him to murder some innocent woman or child later."

"He won't if he can be converted to the Christian faith," Jim insisted firmly.

"A mighty big *if*. But—" The borderman shrugged and took some rawhide thongs from his belt. "We'll leave him tied," he said, and knelt to execute the task. "You fellers grab yer rifles and we'll be startin' fer the fort," he directed.

Joe leaned over one of the forms to detach powder horn and bullet pouch. The sightless eyes made him shrink. He stood in stiff amazement then, as Wetzel calmly scalped the two dead Indians, noticing that Jim turned his face to avoid the spectacle. Wetzel's final act was to pick up Silvertip's beautiful eagle plume, dabble it in a pool of blood, and stick it in the bark of a tree. It was now a challenge and a menace to the Shawnee.

"Come," said the hunter, and led the way into the forest.

Shortly after daylight on the second day following, Wetzel pushed through a thicket of alder and said, "Thar's Fort Henry."

They were on the summit of a mountain from which the land sloped in a long incline until it rose again, abruptly, into a peak higher than the one upon which they stood. The broad Ohio, glistening in the sun, lay at the base of the mountain.

Upon the bluff overlooking the river and under the brow of the mountain, lay the frontier fort. It was a small, low structure, surrounded by a high stockade fence. The watchful, forbidding loopholes, the blackened walls and timbers, spoke of the ten long and bloody years of its history.

They began the descent of the ridge. An hour's rapid walking brought them to the river. Placing his rifle in a clump of willows and directing the boys to do the same, the hunter splashed into the water. They followed him, wading a hundred yards before they neared the island which they now saw hid the fort. Wetzel swam the remaining distance, and climbing the bank, looked back for the boys. They were close behind him. Then he hurried across the island, perhaps a quarter of a mile in width.

"We've a long swim here," he said, waving his hand toward the river's main channel.

The crossing was made without difficulty and, on the bank, Wetzel pointed out a large log building.

"Thar's Colonel Zane in the door," he said.

As they neared the building several men joined the one Wetzel had identified as the colonel. Presently Colonel Zane left the group and came toward them. He was a handsome man in the prime of life.

"What luck, Lew?" he greeted the hunter.

"Not much. Treed five Injuns. Two got away," replied Wetzel.

"Lads, welcome to Fort Henry," said the colonel, smiling. "The rest of your party arrived safely—they'll be overjoyed to see you."

"Colonel Zane, I had a letter from my uncle to you," said Jim, "but the Indians took that and everything else we had with us."

"Never mind. I knew your uncle—your father, too. Come in and change those wet clothes." Colonel Zane turned to Joe. "You've got an ugly knock on the head—who gave you that?"

"Jim Girty. He was with a party of Delawares who ran across us while they were searching for Wetzel."

"Girty with the Delawares!" exclaimed Zane. "There'll be the devil to pay now! But tell me—how did Girty come to strike you?"

"I pulled his nose."

"You did? By George, that's great! But come in and get comfortable—your packs came safely on Jeff's raft and you'll find them inside."

Joe saw an Indian standing a little apart from the other men. He was a manly-looking, dignified redskin.

"Me friend," he said, appearing to read Joe's thoughts.

"That's my Shawnee guide, Tomepomehala," said the colonel. "He's a good fellow, though Jonathan and Wetzel say the only good Indian is a dead one. Come right in here—there are your packs, and you'll find water outside the door."

He led the brothers into a small room, brought out their packs, and left them. He came back shortly with a couple of soft towels.

"Now you lads fix up a bit, then come out and meet my family and tell us all about your adventure. By then dinner will be ready."

The boys lost no time changing into dry clothes. Once dressed and shaved, they were twins again, in costume and feature. By brushing his hair down on his forehead, Joe managed to conceal his discolored bump.

"Looking forward to seeing a charming girl?" smiled Jim.

"Look here, Jim," Joe replied seriously. "Nell might better get someone like you—"

"Absurd!" Jim protested.

"Well, don't you admire her?"

"Well, yes—but—"

"Then go and win her," Joe urged.

"Come, we must find Colonel Zane," said Jim, refusing to continue the subject.

They went out into a hallway which opened into

the yard as well as the large room through which the colonel had first led them. As Jim, in the lead, passed into the room, Nell entered. She ran directly to Jim.

"Oh, Joe!" she whispered.

"You're mistaken again," he replied. "I'm Jim."

For a moment they stared into each other's eyes. Then Colonel Zane's cheery voice rang out.

"Ah, here's Nell and— Now, lads, tell me which is which?"

"That's Jim and I'm Joe," replied Joe.

He greeted Nell naturally and then found himself listening to the congratulations of a number of people. He remembered the names of Mrs. Zane, Silas Zane, and Major McCulloch. Then he found himself looking at the most beautiful girl he had ever seen.

"This is my sister, Mrs. Alfred Clarke—once Betty Zane, and the heroine of Fort Henry," said Colonel Zane proudly, his arm around the slender, dark-eyed girl.

"I would brave the Indians and the wilderness again for this pleasure," said Joe gallantly as he bent low over her hand.

His pretty wife assuring him that dinner was ready, the colonel then led the way into the adjoining room.

During the meal, Colonel Zane questioned his guests about their journey and the treatment they had received at the hands of the Indians. He smiled at Jim's earnestness about converting the red men and laughed when Joe confessed that he had come to the frontier because it was too slow at home.

"Your desire for excitement will soon be satisfied, if it hasn't been already," said the colonel. "I'm not so sure as to your brother's hopes. Still, the Moravian missionaries have accomplished wonders. I visited the Village of Peace not so long ago and was impressed with the friendliness and industry I found there. But it is too early to be sure of its permanent success. The Indian is naturally roving and restless.

"On the whole, though, I think that if the Indians are honestly treated they will return good for good. There are bad ones, of course, but men like the Girtys have caused most of the trouble on the frontier. Jonathan and Wetzel tell me the Shawnees and Chippewas have taken the warpath again. And the Girtys being with the Delawares is reason for alarm. Did you boys learn to what tribe your captors belong?"

"No," Joe replied.

"How did they wear their scalp locks?"

"Their heads were closely shaved, with the exception of a little place on top. The rest of the hair was twisted into a tuft, tied tightly, with a couple of painted pins thrust into it."

"You'll make a woodsman, that's sure!" the colonel exclaimed. "They were Shawnees on the warpath. Mr. Wells seemed anxious to resume his journey down the river, but I'll try to persuade him to stay here awhile. Indeed, I'd like to keep you all here at Fort Henry until this trouble is over—especially the girls."

"We have come prepared for anything," said Kate with a quiet smile. "Our home was with Uncle and our duty is with him."

"You are right, and I hope you'll find a happy home here," rejoined Colonel Zane. "Betty, show the girls your pets and Indian trinkets. I'm going to take the boys to Silas's cabin to see Mr. Wells and then show them over the fort."

As they went out Joe saw the Indian guide standing in exactly the same position as when they had entered.

"He's a fine-looking fellow," Joe remarked as they walked along, "but I don't like him—I guess I'm prejudiced."

"You'll learn to like Tome, as we call him," Colonel Zane reassured him.

As they rounded the corner of the cabin Joe noticed many small, round holes in the logs. He thrust his knife blade into one, and out rolled a leaden ball.

"I'd like to have been here when these were made," he said.

"Well," the colonel laughed, "*I* wished I was back on the Potomac at the time."

They found the old missionary on the doorstep of the adjacent cabin. After greeting the boys warmly he told Colonel Zane he was getting impatient at the delay.

"Mr. Wells, I'm afraid you underrate the danger of your job."

"I fear nothing but the Lord," answered the old man.

"But do you not fear for those with you?" the colonel went on gravely. "It's a long trip to the village, and the way is beset with dangers of which you have no idea. Stay here for a few weeks, or at least until my scouts can report."

"Thank you, Colonel, but I must go."

"Then I beg you to remain a few days, until Jonathan and Wetzel can go with you. If anyone can guide you safely to the Village of Peace, it is they."

At this moment two men approached from the fort. One was Wetzel and the other, who was as tall as Wetzel if not as heavy and muscular, was introduced as the colonel's brother, Jonathan Zane. They conversed quietly with Colonel Zane for a few minutes.

"We'll take two canoes, day after tomorrow," Jonathan said decisively. "Do we have a good rifle for Wetzel?"

"He may have mine," said the old missionary. "I have no use for a weapon with which to destroy God's creatures."

He went into the cabin and came out presently with a long rifle. Wetzel balanced the gun in his hands. It was fully six feet long. The barrel was large, the dark steel finely polished. The stock was black walnut, silver-trimmed. Using Jonathan's powder flask and bullet pouch, Wetzel carefully loaded the weapon, adjusted the flint, dropped a few grains of powder in the pan, and looked around for a mark at which to shoot.

"There, Lew—there's a good shot," said Colonel Zane, pointing toward the river. "Pretty far, even for you, when you don't know the gun."

Joe saw the end of a log, about the size of a man's head, sticking out of the water perhaps a hundred and fifty yards distant. He heard the colonel tell several men who had joined the group that the hunter intended to shoot at a turtle on the log. Straining his eyes, Joe succeeded in distinguishing a small lump on the log.

Wetzel took a step forward, raising the long rifle. The instant it reached a level a thread of flame burst forth, followed by a clear ringing report.

"Did he hit?" Colonel Zane asked eagerly.

"I allow he did," answered Jonathan.

"I'll go and see," Joe offered. He ran down the bank, along the beach, and stepped on the log. There lay a turtle about the size of a saucer. Picking it up, he saw a bullet hole in the shell, and carried it back to the waiting group.

Wetzel examined the dead turtle without speaking. Finally a brief smile crossed his features and he turned to the old missionary.

"I thank ye fer the rifle," he said.

CHAPTER EIGHT

GETTING ACQUAINTED

Leaving Jim with Mr. Wells, Colonel Zane and Joe returned to the cabin. There Joe expressed an eagerness to hear everything the colonel could tell him about Lew Wetzel.

"Well," was the answer, "Lew and I were boys together, so I probably know him better than any man living. Back in Virginia, where he was born, he was like any of the lads, except stronger and quicker. When he was about eighteen a band of marauding Delawares burned the Wetzel homestead and murdered the father, mother, two sisters, and a baby brother. The shock nearly killed Lew, and he was very ill for some time. When he recovered he went after his brothers, Martin and John, who were hunting, and brought them back to their ruined home. Over the ashes the brothers swore eternal vengeance. Since then, a matter of some twenty years, they have been fighting Indians. Lew has saved—actually *saved* —this fort and settlement a score of times."

"Doesn't he do anything but hunt Indians?"

"That is all he lives for. He spends very little time in the settlement. Then he is very quiet, seldom talks unless spoken to. When the passion to hunt Indians comes upon him he seems fierce, almost frenzied. The Indians call him *Atelang*—Deathwind, in English."

"By George! That's what Silvertip said in French —*Le Vent de la Mort.*"

"That's right. A French fur trader gave Wetzel that name years ago, and it has stuck. The Indians say the Deathwind blows through the forest whenever Wetzel is on their trail."

"Colonel Zane, I heard that wind blow through the forest," whispered Joe, and told the story of the night that Wetzel had rescued them.

"Jonathan told me the same sort of thing once," admitted the colonel. "He had been hunting with Wetzel and they separated. During the night Jonathan heard the wind, and the next day he ran across a dead Indian. He believes Wetzel makes the noise, and so do the hunters. I think it may simply be the night wind moaning through the trees."

"I tried to think it was that, but I didn't succeed very well," said Joe. "Anyhow, I knew Wetzel the moment I saw him, just as Jeff Lynn said I would."

"Lew stands alone among all the border scouts and hunters. The Indians have good reason to fear him. He is stronger and speedier than any man, white or red, I've ever known or heard of."

"How long have you been here, Colonel?"

"Twelve years, and a little more—and it's been

one long and continuous fight all that time."

"I'm afraid I'm too late for the fun," said Joe with a quiet laugh.

"Not by another dozen years," replied the colonel, studying Joe's face. "I advise you to learn the ways of the hunters; watch someone skilled in woodcraft. Perhaps Wetzel himself will take you in hand."

Joe glowed at the suggestion. "Dare I ask him?"

"I may be able to arrange it. Now come over to Metzar's place; I want you to meet him. These boys have been cutting timber and have just come in for dinner."

Colonel Zane introduced Joe to five sturdy youths and left him in their company. Sitting down on a log by the cabin, Joe looked them over. They were all light-haired and bronzed-faced, and while not very large they looked strong. In their turn they carefully observed Joe.

"Fine weather we're havin'," said Dick Metzar.

"Fine," Joe agreed.

"Hear ye got ketched by some Shawnees," remarked another youth.

"Was captive for three days," Joe answered.

"Knock any redskins over?" came the query, and Joe saw that they were all looking at him now. It came to him that the question was designed to draw him out, if he was a boaster.

"I was scared speechless most of the time," he said with a smile.

"By gosh, I don't blame ye!" burst out Will Metzar. "Happened t' me oncet, and that's plenty."

They all laughed and looked at Joe in a more friendly manner. While his new friends were eating Joe strolled over to where Colonel Zane sat on his doorstep.

"How did you get on with the boys?" he was asked.

"All right, I hope. Colonel, I'd like to talk to your Indian guide."

Colonel Zane obligingly called over to the guide, who stood near, and Tome came to them. The colonel spoke several sentences rapidly in the Indian tongue and pointed to Joe.

"How do—shake," said Tome, extending his hand. Joe smiled and returned the friendly grip.

"Shawnee ketch?" asked the Indian.

Joe nodded while Colonel Zane spoke once more in Shawnee, explaining the cause of Silvertip's enmity.

"Shawnee chief bad Injun," Tome answered gravely. "Silvertip mad—thunder-mad. Ketch paleface, scalp sure." Having given this warning, Tome stalked back to his position near the corner of the cabin.

"He speaks English quite well," Joe commented.

"Some of the Indians speak the language easily," said the colonel. "My brother's wife, for instance—she is a Huron girl."

"Your brother married an Indian?" Joe was plainly surprised.

"He did, and she is a most beautiful girl. Isaac was a captive among the Hurons for ten years. The chief's daughter, Myeerah, fell in love with him, saved him from being put to death, and they married."

"Well!" Joe was silent for a minute. "Where is your brother now?"

"He and Myeerah live with the tribe. They're working hard for peace, and we're now on fairly friendly terms with the Hurons."

"Isn't this Major McCulloch coming from the fort?" queried Joe, as a stalwart frontiersman approached.

The colonel said it was, and Joe ran his eye over the major. His faded buckskin costume, beaded, fringed, and laced, resembled Jonathan's.

He responded to the colonel's word of greeting and nodded pleasantly to Joe.

"Colonel," he said, "my horse is laid up."

"Heard you were going to Short Creek," said Colonel Zane. "Well, you can take one of my horses. But come inside so we can talk over your expedition."

The afternoon passed slowly. Jim and Mr. Wells were absorbed in their plans for the future. Nell and Kate were resting. Joe idled the hours away, watching and listening.

CHAPTER NINE

THE RAISING

That night Joe went to bed determined to rise early the next morning. He had been invited to take part in a "raising," which meant that a new cabin was to be erected—always quite an event in the lives of the settlers.

He was up bright and early, to dress himself in a complete buckskin suit, for which he had traded his cloth garments. He thought he had never been so comfortable in his life before. The soft buckskin was so warm and smooth and its weight so light, the moccasins so well fitting and springy that he wanted to caper about like a frolicsome colt.

When he met the others, however, he tried not to show the joy that he felt in his woodsman's garb. Nell glanced at him shyly; Kate spoke her admiration; Jim joked him in brotherly fashion; Colonel Zane, understanding how he felt, felt warmly drawn toward the boy. He watched Joe, his eyes kind but grave.

The raising brought out the whole settlement. The women looked on and gossiped; the children played; the men labored with the heavy timbers. Joe and the other newcomers watched it all with interest.

"Well, young man, I'm sorry you're to leave us to-night," Colonel Zane remarked as Joe came over to where he and his wife and sister were watching the work.

"Do we travel by night?" Joe asked.

"Oh, yes, it's quite necessary. The plan is to keep along the south shore all night, then cross over at a place called Girty's Point, where you'll stay in hiding during daylight. From there you paddle up Yellow Creek, the portage across country to the head of the Tuscarwawas. Another night's journey will then bring you to the Village of Peace."

Jim and Mr. Wells, with his nieces, now joined the party and all stood watching as the last logs were put in place.

"Colonel Zane, my first log-raising is an education to me," said the young minister earnestly. "There is such good will among these men! Mr. Wells, doesn't it impress you?"

"The pioneers act as brothers together because of the danger they face," said the missionary. "I want to bring this same fine feeling of brotherhood to the Indians."

"I have seen it," said Colonel Zane. "When I came here twelve years ago the Indians were peaceable. If the pioneers had paid for land, as I and a few others did, there would never have been a border war. But the settlers grabbed every acre they could. Then the

Indians rebelled, and the Girtys and their kind spread more discontent, and now the border is blood-stained."

As the party proceeded toward the colonel's cabin, Jim and Nell found themselves side by side. They had not spoken to each other since the day before, when she had mistaken him for Joe.

"Doesn't Joe look fine in his hunting-suit?" asked Jim.

"I really hadn't noticed— Well, yes, he does look nice," she replied.

"Are you angry with him?"

"Certainly not."

"You don't seem to have paid much attention to him since we got here."

"Why should I?" she demanded. "He doesn't seem to be interested in me—any more."

"Joe may be reckless," Jim pressed on, "but his heart is pure gold. Right now he's full of notions about chasing Indians and roaming through the forest, but he'll get over that. He's sure to settle down —especially if you'll help him."

"I will, if he will let me," she said, her eyes shining.

CHAPTER TEN

VILLAGE OF PEACE

Under the blue-black vault of heaven, with its myriads of twinkling stars, the voyagers resumed their westward journey. Warned to absolute silence by their stern guides, they lay back in the canoes and thought and listened.

The frail craft glided into black space, side by side, close under the overhanging willows. Long moments passed into long hours as the guides paddled tirelessly.

With the gray dawn came the careful landing of the canoes, a cold breakfast eaten under cover of a willow thicket, and the beginning of a long day. Hidden from the keen eyes of Indian scouts, they waited for the friendly mantle of night.

The hours dragged until once more the canoes were launched, this time not on the broad Ohio but on a stream that flowed still and somber under dense foliage.

The voyagers did not speak, not even in a whisper. They scarcely moved, so menacing had become the slow, listening caution of Jonathan and Wetzel. A snapping of twigs somewhere in the darkness delayed them for long moments. Every second was heavy with fear.

But finally another dark night wore on to a tardy dawn, and each of its fearful hours meant more miles behind them. The sun was rising in ruddy glory when Wetzel ran his canoe into the bank just ahead of a sharp bend in the stream.

"Do we get out here?" asked Jim, as Jonathan turned his canoe toward Wetzel's.

"The village lies just around the bend," answered the guide, "and since Wetzel cannot go there I'll take you all in my canoe."

"There isn't enough room. I'll wait," Joe said quietly, and he stayed behind with Wetzel while the others proceeded in Jonathan's canoe.

Dozens of canoes lay upon the well-cleared banks. A log bridge spanned the stream. Above the slight ridge of rising ground could be seen the poles of Indian tepees.

As their canoe grated upon the sandy beach, a little Indian boy who had been playing in the shallow water raised his head and smiled. He came running up to them as they landed. Save for tiny buckskin breeches he was naked, his skin gleaming gold-bronze in the sunlight.

"Me Benny," he announced.

With a tender exclamation Nell bent and kissed him.

Jonathan Zane swung his canoe back upstream to

A Little Indian Boy Greeted Them

get Joe. Soon after the trim craft slipped out of sight around the bend its curved nose peeped from behind the willows and it swept back into full view. There was no one in it but the guide.

"Where is Joe?" asked Jim in surprise.

"Gone," was the quiet answer.

"Gone? Didn't Wetzel see him—?"

"They are both gone."

Nell and Jim stared at each other, their faces paling.

"Come, I'll take you to the village," said Jonathan, getting out of his canoe.

"Can't you tell us what it means—this disappearance?" Jim asked anxiously.

"They're gone, canoe and all. I knew Wetzel was goin' but I didn't calkilate the lad'd go with him." The guide would say no more.

When Jim reached the top of the bank he looked around eagerly. In front of him was a plain, in the center of which stood a wide, low structure surrounded by log cabins and an outlying circle of tepees. A number of trees shaded the clearing. The settlement swarmed with Indians. A few shrill halloos uttered by those who first saw the newcomers brought men, women, and children trooping toward the party, all showing friendly curiosity.

Jonathan Zane stopped before a cabin and called in through the open door. A short, stoop-shouldered white man, clad in faded linsey, appeared.

"Mr. Zeisberger, I've fetched a party from Fort Henry," said Jonathan. Then, without another word, he hurried back through the throng of Indians, never turning his dark face to right or left.

"Mr. Wells, welcome to the Village of Peace!" exclaimed Mr. Zeisberger, wringing the old missionary's hand. "I remember you well."

"I'm happy indeed to get here," Mr. Wells answered. "I have brought my two nieces, Nell and Kate, and this young man, James Downs, a minister of God and earnest in his desire to help in our work."

Mr. Zeisberger gave his own room to the girls, assuring them that it was the most "luxurious" in the whole village. It contained a chair, a table, and a bed of Indian blankets and buffalo robes. The girls, weary from the long trip, lay down to rest. Mr. Wells, claiming lack of fatigue, asked his old friend to tell him all about his work.

"We have met with wonderful success—far beyond our fondest dreams," and Mr. Zeisberger launched into a detailed account of the Moravian Mission's efforts.

The work lay chiefly among the Delawares, who seemed to be well disposed toward the white man's religion, on the whole. The missionaries had succeeded in converting many of the eastern Delawares, and ten years ago sixteen canoes, filled with converted Indians and missionaries, drifted down the Allegheny to Fort Pitt, thence down the Ohio to the Big

Beaver, up that stream, and far into the Ohio wilderness.

A settlement was founded here. The news was spread near and far. Red men from all tribes came flocking to the colony. Many doubted, some were converted, all listened. Great excitement arose when one of the wisest chiefs became a convert to the paleface religion.

In a few years this beautiful, prosperous town arose, called the Village of Peace. At first there were only a few wigwams. Then a large log structure was built and used as a church. A school, a mill, and a workshop followed. Fields were cultivated. Horses and cattle grazed on the plain.

The Village of Peace blossomed. The good-fellowship and industry of the converts had a good influence. Bands of traveling Indians, whether friendly or not, were well treated and never went away empty-handed.

One of the most popular things in the village was the church bell. It seemed to charm the Indians. On still nights the savages in distant villages could hear its mellow notes summoning worshipers to evening service.

"You have come at a good time," continued Mr. Zeisberger. "Mr. Edwards and Mr. Young are working to establish other missionary posts. Reverend Heckewelder is coming soon to help in the spreading of our work."

Jim asked how long it would take him to learn the Delaware tongue.

"Not long. However, we have fine interpreters, so it really isn't necessary."

"We heard a great deal at Fort Pitt and Fort Henry about the danger, as well as the uselessness, of our venture," said Jim.

"There are many hostile savages about, but we do not fear them. We invite them. We must convert the wicked as well as the good ones—and we shall succeed."

Jim resolved to go slowly, study the red men's natures, and not preach to them until he had mastered their language. He wanted to bring the real truth to their simple minds clearly and forcibly.

"I hope you have rested well," said Zeisberger as Nell and Kate came into the room.

"Thank you—we feel much better," answered Kate.

They had put on fresh gowns and looked attractive and appealing.

"My, my!" exclaimed Mr. Zeisberger, looking at them appreciatively. "I'm afraid Edwards and Young won't want to leave now!" He turned to include the men: "Come, I will show you the Village of Peace."

"Are all these Indians Christians?" Jim asked.

"Oh, no. The Indians you see here and out there under the shade are not Christians, though they are friendly. Our converts work in the fields or shops."

Jim and the others looked in the door of the large log structure. The floor of the immense room was covered with benches and there was a raised platform at one end. A few windows let in the light. The floor was hard-packed clay; the seats were crude; the platform bore a white-oak cross.

Mr. Zeisberger led them to a cabin. "This is one of our shops, where we make brooms, harness for the horses, farming implements—everything useful that we can."

The interior was a scene of bustling activity. A score of Indians were busily employed. In one corner a brave held a piece of red-hot iron on an anvil while another wielded a sledge hammer. In another corner a circle of men sat around a pile of dried grass and reeds, twisting these materials into baskets. Three Indian carpenters sawed and pounded at a bench. Youths ran back and forth, carrying pails, boards, blocks of wood.

Outside again, the missionary pointed out wide fields of corn and hillsides dotted with browsing cattle, droves of horses, and pens of pigs. The Village of Peace looked prosperous indeed.

Later, Jim walked with Nell by the bank of the stream.

"Joe wanted so much to hunt with Wetzel," he said. "But he will come back—surely he will return to us when he has satisfied his craving for adventure."

"I do not think so," Nell answered solemnly.

"Nell, you don't think he went away deliberately—"

"I think it was just because the wilderness means more to him than you or I do."

"Oh, no," Jim protested. "You don't understand. He really loved you."

"Jim, I hope he loved me," she replied. "His coldness for the last few days has hurt me. If he cared, as you say, I won't be so miserable."

The deep notes of the church bell pealed out, calling the Christians to the evening service.

CHAPTER ELEVEN

THE NEW PREACHER

The drowsy summer days passed peacefully in the mission village. Mr. Wells preached to the Indians every day, using an interpreter. Nell and Kate spent their time in housekeeping and decorating their new home. Jim busied himself in careful study of the customs and habits of the red men.

No trace of Joe had been seen by any of the friendly Indian runners. He had disappeared in the deep forest mazes as completely as any denizen of the wilderness.

Jim spent part of every morning with the interpreters, and was rapidly learning the Delaware language. He went freely among the Indians, trying to win their good will. Soon he was in the good graces of Glickhican, the converted Delaware chief, and talked with the wise old Indian for hours.

From him Jim learned not only the Indians' well-founded reasons for their hatred of the whites who had pushed them from their lands by force and dishonesty but also much of their stories and legends. Through these myths he hoped to get ideas of the Indians' religion.

Glickhican told Jim that not once during his sev-

enty years of life had he ever lied or stolen, that he
had never betrayed a friend or killed a man, except
in self-defense. Gazing at the chief's fine, strong face,
Jim believed him without a shadow of a doubt.

But when he came to study the hostile Indians
who flocked to the village, he was baffled. They were
silent and secretive, like so many sphinxes. They accepted his gifts but it was impossible to tell if they
appreciated them.

Several chiefs came to the village. Among them,
Glickhican pointed out Wingenund, Half-King,
Shingiss, and Kotoxen, all of the Wolf tribe of the
Delawares. Glickhican explained that the Delaware
nation was divided into the Wolf and Turtle tribes,
the former warlike and the latter peaceable. Few of
the Wolf tribe had accepted the new faith. Wingenund himself held a neutral attitude toward the Village of Peace, though his advisers, Pipe and Wish-
tonah, were opposed.

Jim thought over carefully all he had learned. He
wanted to make up a sermon different from any
other they had ever heard. He wanted to tell them
things they would understand.

His first speech to the Indians was made one day
when Mr. Wells was ill and the other missionaries
absent from the village. He spoke simply and earnestly, telling them the thoughts which had come to
him while he had been living among them. He was
friendly and sincere.

The converts among the Indians were deeply moved. The others seemed silent and thoughtful. Every day he was called upon to speak, and every day at least one savage stepped forward to say that he wanted to become a Christian. Each day, too, the crowd grew larger. Finally no one but Jim preached at the afternoon meetings.

The news spread rapidly. The Village of Peace entertained more red men than ever before. The Christian faith gained an ever stronger foothold. Heckewelder, the leader of the western Moravian Mission, visited the village and arranged a three-day religious festival. Indian runners were sent with invitations to all the tribes. They were asked to come, share in the feasts, and listen to the white man's teaching.

CHAPTER TWELVE

"DO NOT BURY THE HATCHET!"

From dawn until noon on Sunday bands of Indians arrived at the Village of Peace. Hundreds of canoes glided down the stream and bumped their prows into the pebbly bank. Groups of warriors rode out of the forests into the clearing. Squaws carrying papooses, maidens bearing baskets, and children of all ages came along every trail.

Gifts were presented during the morning. Then the visitors feasted. In the afternoon all gathered in the grove to listen to the preaching.

Heckewelder, a tall, spare man, arranged the seating. The converted Indians were just behind the knoll on which the speaker was to stand. In a half circle facing the knoll were the chieftains and head men of the different tribes. He then made a short speech about the work of the mission, what had already been done and what good it still hoped to do. Then he introduced Jim.

Jim looked into a thousand dark, still faces. Eagle plumes quivered in the soft breeze. In front of him sat fifty chiefs, solemn and dignified. Many of them were renowned in war, noted for their bravery and cunning.

Hepote, a chief who was supposed never to have listened to the words of a paleface, was in the center. Beside him sat Shausoto and Pipe, both unmoving foes of the white man. Wingenund stood at the extreme left of the circle, leaning against a maple. He wore a long mantle trimmed with white and a heavy gold bracelet circled one bronzed arm.

At his feet sat his daughter, Whispering Winds. She raised her soft black eyes expectantly to the young missionary's face.

As Jim looked out over the sea of faces he started in surprise. A sudden glance of fiery eyes had caught his attention. He recognized Silvertip, the Shawnee chief. He sat motionless on a powerful black horse—it was Joe's thoroughbred, Lance. But he had no time to spend thinking of Joe's enemy. He began his speech.

"Chieftains, warriors, people of the forest, listen. I have come to tell you of the Great Spirit of the white man. As many moons ago as the blades of grass that grow on the plain the Great Spirit made the world. He made the lakes and rivers, the plains and tangled forests, over which He caused the sun to shine and the rain to fall. He gave life to the elk, the deer, the bear, the fox—all the beasts and birds and fishes. He created the first man, and from this man's rib He made the first woman so that the man would have a mate.

"Life was fair in the beautiful forest. There was

plenty of food for the man and woman to eat, but there was one tree whose fruit the Great Spirit commanded them not to eat. But a serpent tempted the woman to eat this fruit, and the woman in turn persuaded the man to eat some. So the Great Spirit drove the man and the woman from the beautiful forest. They went far away to learn to live as best they could. From them all tribes descended.

"Many moons ago the Great Spirit sorrowed to see the tribe of palefaces living in ignorance and sin. So He sent His only son to save them and to teach them a better way to live. If they listened and believed and taught the other tribes they would be welcomed back to the beautiful forest.

"Many of the palefaces believed and followed the new ways. The Great Spirit was pleased and told them to go afar and teach all the other tribes.

"The Great Spirit of whom I teach and the one in whom you believe are the same. The happy hunting grounds of the Indian and the beautiful forest of the white man are the same. The paleface and the red man are one.

"The Indian knows the habits of the beaver; he can follow the forest paths and guide his canoe through the foaming rapids; he is honest and brave, but he is not wise. He worships the trees and rocks, but these things do not live, they have no spirit. The spirit is only in his own heart. It guides the arrow and steers the canoe. It is a piece of the Great Spirit.

"Red men, you must learn to make your spirit do good deeds. This is what it means to be a Christian. A Christian loves the Great Spirit. If you love the Great Spirit you will love your wives, your children, your friends, even your foes. You will love the palefaces. No more will you wage war. You will wear your knife and tomahawk only when you hunt for meat. When your days are done you will meet all your loved ones again in the beautiful forest. There peace will dwell forever.

"Comrades, be wise. Forget the wicked palefaces, who sell firewater and lie and steal and kill. If those palefaces do not change they will never go back to the beautiful forest. You have much to forgive, but if you forgive you will please the Great Spirit.

"Look at this Village of Peace! Once it contained few, but now there are many. Here we have cabins and horses and cattle and much corn. Plenty has come to those who believe in the Great Spirit and do as He says. The Christian Indians are happy. They are at peace with the red man and with the paleface. Their children will walk hand in hand with the palefaces.

"Do not let bitterness stay in your hearts. It is serpent poison. Forgive the palefaces who have robbed you of your lands. Then peace will come. Love these Christian Indians, love the missionaries—as they love you; love all living creatures.

"Brothers, the paleface teacher begs you. Think

of what will come. The paleface will not steal a Christian's land. The evil paleface will not dare to invade the Village of Peace. The Great Spirit smiles on those who love Him and love their fellow men."

An impressive silence fell on the great crowd as Jim finished. Then an aged Delaware chief arose.

"Netawatwees is almost persuaded to be a Christian," he said, facing the other Indians.

Another quiet period followed before another old chieftain got up.

"White Eyes is the oldest chief of the Lenni-Lenape. Now that he draws near the evening of his life he is glad that wisdom has come before the sun has set. White Eyes believes the young White Father. The red man does not have to forget the happy hunting grounds to love the palefaces' god. White Eyes bids his people listen to the White Father. War is wrong. Peace is best. Love is the way to peace. White Eyes has spoken."

The old chief slowly walked toward the Christian Indians. He laid aside his knife and tomahawk, took off his eagle plumes and war bonnet, and, bareheaded, sat down among the converted red men.

Amid breathless silence Wingenund advanced toward the knoll. His dark eyes swept over the glade.

"Wingenund's ears have heard a soft-voiced thrush. Now Wingenund thunders to his people, to his friends, to the chiefs of other tribes: *Do not bury the hatchet!* The young White Father's tongue runs smooth like the gliding brook. Listen—but wait! Let time prove his beautiful tale.

"Wingenund has grown old among his warriors. He loves them. He fears for them. The dream of the paleface is too beautiful to come true. Long ago the red men lived in peace and happiness. Then the paleface came with his ax, firewater, his guns, and the peace of the red men has gone.

"Wingenund does not tell his braves to fight. He is sick of bloodshed. But he asks his people to wait. The gifts of the paleface always contain a poisoned arrow. When Wingenund can cross unarmed to the Big Water he will change his mind. When Death-wind's bloody trail has ended Wingenund will believe."

CHAPTER THIRTEEN

THE FACE AT THE WINDOW

The summer waned, and each succeeding day held more of autumn in it. The little colony of whites in the Village of Peace took small note of the changing season, busy as they were.

Upward of fifty Indians, several of them important chiefs, had become converted since Jim began preaching. Heckewelder declared it to be a wonderful showing. He had persuaded the tribes west of the Village of Peace to let him establish two other missionary posts in that region, and with his two helpers, Young and Edwards, he had made several journeys to these places, preaching and making gifts.

A rivalry had developed between Young and Edwards over Kate Wells. They were both good, honest men, still young, but two homelier men could hardly have been found. Further, they were both awkward in the presence of a woman—happy, foolish, and speechless whenever Kate was around.

Heckewelder could not hide his amusement and Nell did not try very hard to conceal hers, but Kate never let a suspicion of it escape her. She remained kind and gracious to both of the men. However, one day Heckewelder seemed to lose his patience.

"Say, you two are becoming more ornamental than useful!" he exploded. "All this changing of coats and trimming of mustaches and sighing doesn't seem to have affected the young lady. I've a notion to send you both to Maumee town, a hundred miles away. I admit the young lady is charming, but if she continues to hinder the work of this mission I must object. Settle it—you both can't marry her, so settle it!"

On the afternoon following this outburst Hecke-welder took Mr. Wells to one of the Indian shops and Jim and Nell went canoeing. Young and Edwards, after considerable hemming and hawing, determined to settle the question.

Young was a pale, thin man, nervous and timid in manner. Edwards was his opposite, a heavy-set, ro-bust fellow, with a round face and a rather self-confident bearing—except when there was a woman near him.

"Dave, I couldn't ask her," said Young, trembling at the very thought. "Besides, there's no hope for me—what would such a glorious creature as Kate see in a puny thing like me?"

"George, you're not over-handsome," admitted Edwards, shaking his head. "But you never can tell about women. Don't be too scared about asking her. Besides, you might make it easier for me. You know —tell her about me, sort of prepare the way, so I—"

"No, I couldn't," gasped Young, falling into a

chair and turning even paler. "I couldn't ask her to accept me, let alone do another man's wooing. She thinks more of you—she'll accept you."

"You really think so?" Edwards asked nervously.

"Of course. You're such a fine figure of a man! She'll take you—and I'll be glad. All this fretting around and worrying has about finished me. Go—hurry, and get it over with!"

"Yes, we *must* get it settled," replied Edwards, getting up with a brave effort. "You're sure she—cares for me?" he faltered.

"Yes, yes—I *know* she does! Go along—hurry—I tell you I can't stand this any longer," cried Young, pushing him out of the door.

Edwards clung to the door frame. "You—won't go first?" he whispered.

"I won't go at all! I couldn't ask her! I don't want her! Go!"

As Edwards started reluctantly toward the adjoining cabin Young flung himself on his bed. What a relief to feel it was all over! He lay for hours, it seemed.

Finally Edwards came back in. Young leaped to his feet and saw his friend stumbling over a chair, a miserable expression on his face.

"Well?" cried Young sharply.

"She—she refused me," faltered Edwards. "She was very sweet and kind—said something about being my sister—but she wouldn't have me."

"What did you say to her?" Young demanded, almost paralyzed by hope.

"I told her everything I could think of," replied Edwards despondently. "Even what you said—about how she cared for me—that you were sure of it, and that you didn't want her—"

"*You jackass!*" roared Young. He rushed out of the cabin and a moment later stood wild-eyed before Kate.

"Did that fool say I didn't love you?" he demanded.

Kate looked up, startled. Then, realizing what was wrong, she resumed her usual calmness.

"If you mean Mr. Edwards, yes, he did say as much. I gathered that he had monopolized all the love in the vicinity of the Village of Peace."

"But it's not true—I do love you—I've loved you ever since I first saw you—I told Dave that—Heckewelder knows it—everybody knows it—even the Indians—" Young cried in desperation.

Kate gazed at him with wide eyes.

"Of course," he went on, "I know you don't care for me—"

"Did Mr. Edwards tell you so?" she asked quietly.

"Why—yes, he's often said he thought that. He always seemed to think he was the object of your affections—and I believed he was, too."

"But it's not true," Kate said.

"What's not true?"

"About—my not caring."

"Kate!" Overcome, Young fell over a chair in his eagerness to reach her side. On his knees, he grasped her hand and kissed it.

"It's been you all the time." Kate smiled.

"Look here, Downs," said Heckewelder to Jim one evening; "come to the door—see there."

Somewhat surprised, Jim got up from the supper table and went to the door. He saw two tall Indians walking to and fro under the maples. It was still light enough for him to see clearly.

"Silvertip—and Girty!" he exclaimed.

"Girty I knew, of course, but I wasn't sure who the other was," said Heckewelder, drawing Jim into another room.

"What are they up to?" Jim asked apprehensively.

"I don't know. Girty has been here several times lately. I saw him conferring with Pipe at Goshocking. I'm afraid there's some deviltry afoot."

Later the entire missionary party gathered in Mr. Wells's room.

"Next Wednesday I will perform the great ceremony," remarked Heckewelder, laying a kindly hand on Young's shoulder and smiling at Kate. "We'll celebrate the first white wedding in the Village of Peace."

Young looked down at his boots and blushed. Edwards coughed loudly to hide his embarrassment.

Kate smiled gently. Nell's eyes twinkled and she was about to speak when Heckewelder continued:

"I hope I'll have another wedding on my hands before long."

Nell turned swiftly away and looked out of the window, her cheeks flaming. Jim frowned and bit his lip. Edwards began to laugh.

Suddenly they all jumped as Nell gave utterance to a shuddering scream: "Oh-h-h!"

They all gazed at her in amazement. Every bit of color had left her face. Her eyes wide in horror, she relaxed her grip on the window sill and staggered back into the middle of the room as if she were dizzy.

Heckewelder ran to the door to look out while the others gathered around the girl, who seemed on the brink of fainting. Her eyelids fluttered, then opened wide as she stared speechless at her friends.

"Nell, what is it—what frightened you so?" asked Kate anxiously.

"Oh!" gasped Nell. "I—I was looking out the window into the dark—and suddenly I saw a face, a *terrible* face! It was right by the window—I could have touched it— A greedy, wolfish face, with a long, hooked nose. It was that white man—that awful white man; I never saw him before, but I knew him!"

"Girty," said Heckewelder, who had returned quietly. "Well, calm yourself, girl; he has gone."

The incident worried them all and made them nervous for several days. However, nothing more

Nell Gave a Shuddering Scream

was seen of Girty and gradually they forgot about it.

Kate's wedding day dawned. Early in the afternoon Jim and Nell accompanied her and Young into the woods near the clearing to gather wild flowers with which to decorate the cabin.

After he and Nell had walked a little way in silence, Jim said, "I hope—I pray Joe comes back, but if he doesn't—Nell, won't you care for me?"

"Jim, let's not speak of it now," she whispered. Then she turned to the others. "Here are some nice clusters of clematis and goldenrod—let's pick all we can."

The two men had almost buried the girls under huge masses of the flowers when the soft tread of moccasined feet caused them to turn in surprise. Six savages stood waist-deep in the bushes. Fierce, painted faces scowled from behind leveled rifles.

There was a snapping of twigs and two other figures came into view—Girty and Silvertip.

"Don't yell," Girty warned, "or I'll leave ye layin' here fer the buzzards."

He stepped forward and grasped Young, speaking in the Indian language and pointing to a near-by tree. While one of the Indians began to tie Young to the tree Girty turned to look at the girls.

"I been layin' fer you," he said to Nell. "Purtiest gal I ever seed on the border. Arter I've fed yer mealy-mouth preacher t' the buzzards mebbe you'll larn to love me."

CHAPTER FOURTEEN

DEATHWIND'S PUPIL

Not many miles from the Village of Peace rose an irregular chain of hills, the first indication of the Appalachian mountain system. There were ridges thickly wooded with white oak, poplar, and hickory, with here and there a towering sentinel pine. There were clefts in the hills, passes lined by gray-stoned cliffs, below which ran clear brooks.

One of these valleys was so narrow that the sun seldom brightened the brook that ran along its floor. The head of the valley tapered so that the walls nearly met. This lonely nook was deep and dark and cool. Everywhere was a soft, fresh, bright green. Ferns and moss covered the old gray cliffs. Under a great shelving rock was a dewy dell into which sunshine never struck.

Along the flower-bordered stream a tall young man, carrying a rifle, walked cautiously, peering into the branches overhead. A gray flash shot along the limb of a white oak.

The rifle was raised, then lowered. The hunter walked around the tree. Presently, up under the tree-top, snug under a knotty limb, he spied a ball of gray fur. Grasping a branch of underbrush, he shook it vigorously. The threshing sound caused the squirrel to slip from his retreat and stick his nose over the limb.

Crack!

With a scratching and tearing of bark, the squirrel loosened his hold and then fell, hitting the ground with a thump. As the hunter picked up his quarry a streak of sunshine glinting through the leaves brightened his face.

It was Joe Downs.

He shouldered his rifle and went back up the ravine. Presently a dull roar sounded above the babble of the brook. Passing under the cliff, Joe turned around a rocky corner and came to an abrupt end of the ravine. A waterfall marked the spot where the brook entered.

Upon a flat rock, so near the waterfall that spray flew over him, sat another hunter.

"I heered four shots," he said as Joe came up.

"I got a squirrel for every shot," Joe answered.

Wetzel led the way along a narrow trail which gradually wound toward the brink of the ravine. The path emerged some distance above the falls at the top of the bluff, ran along the edge a few yards, and took a course back into a densely wooded thicket.

Before stepping out on the open cliff Wetzel paused and peered keenly around in all directions. No living thing was to be seen. The silence was the deep unbroken calm of the wilderness.

Wetzel stepped to the bluff and looked over. The stony wall opposite was only thirty feet away and somewhat lower than on this side. Once a band of Indians, pursuing the hunter into this fastness, had come out on this bluff and marveled at what they thought Wetzel's prowess, believing that he had eluded them by making a wonderful leap.

Now Wetzel crouched and swung himself down over the edge of the bluff. Joe followed suit. They dropped onto a narrow ledge about ten feet below. At one end of this ledge grew a hardy ironwood shrub. Above it a scrub pine leaned out over the ravine.

Laying his rifle down, Wetzel grasped a strong root and cautiously slid over the side. When all of his body but his sinewy fingers had disappeared, they loosened their hold on the root, grasped the rifle, and dragged it down out of sight.

With similar care, Joe took hold of the same root, let himself down, and when at full length swung himself in under the ledge. His feet found a pocket in the cliff. Letting go of the root, he took hold of his rifle and in another second was safe.

Of all Wetzel's retreats—and he had many—he considered this one the safest. One day, hotly pursued by Shawnees, he had been headed off on this cliff and had let himself down on the ledge, intending to drop from it to the tops of the trees below. Taking advantage of every little aid, he swung over by

means of the shrub and was about to leap when he
saw that the cliff shelved under the ledge, while
within reach of his feet was the entrance to a cave.

He found the cave to be small, with an opening at
the back into a split in the rock. Evidently the rear
entrance was used by bears, for whom the cave served
as a winter sleeping quarters. Thus Wetzel had a
hiding place where it was next to impossible to locate
him. He kept the retreat, which he always entered
by the cliff and left by the rear opening, well pro-
visioned.

When they were satisfied that all was well within
their refuge, Joe laid aside his rifle, and whistling
softly, began to prepare supper. The back part of
the cave was high enough so that he could stand
erect and roomy enough to be comfortable. There
was a neat little stone fireplace and several cooking
utensils and gourds. A pile of wood and a bundle of
pine cones lay in one corner. Haunches of dried beef,
bear, and buffalo meat hung from pegs. A bag of
parched corn and one of dried apples lay on a rocky
shelf. Near by hung a powder horn filled with salt
and pepper. In the cleft back of the cave was a spring
of clear, cold water.

Joe and Wetzel enjoyed the simple meal as they
never would have enjoyed a feast. As the evening
shadows entered the cave, Wetzel lighted his pipe
and Joe settled down to rest in comfort.

Wetzel had taken a liking to Joe while he was

leading him and his brother to Fort Henry. Following events had strengthened that liking, and now that Joe had followed him into the forest a strong affection had developed between them.

Wetzel understood Joe's burning desire to roam the forest, though he half expected the boy would soon tire of this roving life. But now they had been in the woods for weeks, and every day Joe had showed his mettle in some way. Wetzel finally admitted him to the secrets of his favorite hiding-place. The days passed swiftly then, with the man and the boy growing ever closer to each other.

Wetzel had hunted with Jonathan Zane but he had never known a real companion or friend. His feeling for Joe was something new. Joe was happy and enthusiastic, yet his good spirits never jarred on the hunter. The boy was apt, he forgot nothing, he had the eye of a born woodsman, and—what impressed Wetzel the most—he was as strong and supple as a young lynx and absolutely fearless.

Tonight the hunter was more silent than usual and Joe, healthily sleepy, lay down on a bed of fragrant boughs. Wetzel sat in the deepening gloom, puffing at his pipe and occasionally glancing at the boy, whose deep, even breathing indicated that he slept.

He knew that Colonel Zane had taken a liking to the boy and had offered him work and a home. He had also noticed the warm light in Nell's eyes when she looked at Joe. He felt strangely softened at the thought of this boy who had chosen to share his lonely wilderness life.

Joe was awakened by the chirp of the chipmunk that every morning ran along the seamy wall of the opposite side of the gorge. Getting up, he went to the back of the cave, where he found Wetzel combing out his long hair. Thrusting his hands into the icy pool, Joe bathed his face.

Joe understood why Wetzel took such pains in caring for his long hair. If he cut it off it would seem that he feared the Indians, for they had long coveted that streaming black mane and had sworn to take it. It would make any brave a famous chief.

After breakfast Wetzel said to Joe, "You stay here while I look around some. Mebbe I'll come back soon and we'll go out and kill a buffler. Injuns sometimes foller up a buffler trail and I want to be sure none of 'em are chasin' that herd we saw."

Wetzel left the cave by the rear. It took him fifteen minutes to crawl to the end of the winding, stony passage. Lifting the stone which closed up the opening, he peered out and listened. Then rising, he replaced the stone and passed down the wooded hillside.

It was a beautiful morning. The dew glistened on the leaves, the sun shone bright and warm, and the birds sang in the trees. The hunter's moccasins pressed so gently on the moss and leaves that they made no more sound than the soft tread of a panther. His trained ear was alert to catch any unfamiliar noise; his keen eyes sought first the more remote open glades and glens, then dropped to the mossy bluff beneath his feet. Fox squirrels dashed away from before him into bushy retreats, grouse whirred away into thickets, startled deer snorted and loped off with their white flags upraised.

Wetzel circled back over the hill, took a long survey from a rocky eminence, and then scouted the lowland for several miles. He located the herd of buffalo and satisfied himself there were no Indians near—the bison were grazing quietly. Then he returned to the cave, where a soft whistle into the back entrance told Joe that the hunter was waiting.

"Coast clear?" whispered the boy, thrusting his head out.

The hunter nodded and, snuggling his rifle into the hollow of his arm, proceeded down the hill. Joe followed closely, trying, as Wetzel had trained him, to take each step precisely in the hunter's footprints. Halfway down the hill, Wetzel paused.

"See anythin'?" he whispered.

Joe glanced around in all directions. Many mistakes had taught him to be cautious. He could make out nothing but the colors of the woods, the gray of the tree trunks and, in the openings through the forest green, the dead purple haze of forests farther on. He smiled and shook his head at the hunter.

"Try again. Dead ahead," whispered Wetzel.

Joe directed his gaze on a clump of sassafras a hundred feet ahead. He searched the open places, the shadows—even the branches. Then he turned his eyes slowly to the right. Suddenly his eye became fixed on a small object protruding from behind a beech tree. It was pointed, and in color darker than the gray bark of the tree.

"That's a buck's ear," he said.

Hardly had he finished speaking when Wetzel intentionally snapped a twig. Out into the open glade bounded a large buck with a whistle of alarm. Joe's rifle came up to cover the bounding deer but the hunter struck up the weapon.

"Don't kill fer the sake o' killin', lad," he said quietly. "We have plenty of venison. We'll go arter a buffler—I've a hankerin' fer a good rump steak."

Half an hour later they emerged from the forest into a wide plain of waving grass. It was an oval-shaped valley, encircled by hills. Joe saw a herd of large animals browsing in a meadow. His heart beat faster—surely he would get a shot at one of these huge fellows.

Wetzel told Joe to do exactly as he did, then dropped on hands and knees and began to crawl through the long grass. Joe followed him with difficulty, for the hunter crawled as fast as he walked. At length the borderman paused.

"We near enough?" Joe whispered.

"Nope. Jest circlin' on 'em. Wind's not right and I'm afeered they'll get our scent."

Wetzel rose carefully to peep over the top of the grass, then dropped on all fours again and resumed his advance. Joe wondered how those wide shoulders pushed through the weeds and grass stems without even seeming to shake them.

"Flat now," whispered Wetzel, putting his broad hand on Joe's back and pressing him down. "Now's yer time fer good practice. Trail yer rifle over yer back—if ye're keerful it won't slide off—and reach out fer with one arm and dig yer fingers in deep. Then pull yerself forrard."

Wetzel slipped through the grass like a huge snake. His long, lithe body wormed its way among the reeds. But for Joe it was difficult work. The dry reeds broke under him and the stalks of grass trembled and shook. He worked hard at it, learning all the while, improving with each rod.

"We're near enough," whispered Wetzel, stopping behind a bush. He rose and surveyed the plain, then motioned to Joe to look.

Joe raised himself to his knees. His heart leaped. Not fifty yards away was a great, shaggy buffalo. He was the king of the herd, but ill at ease, pawing the grass and shaking his huge head. Near him were several cows and a half-grown calf. Beyond was the main herd, extending as far as Joe could see—a great sea of black humps.

"Pick out the little feller—the reddish-brown one —and plug him behind the shoulder. Shoot close now."

Joe raised his rifle. He had covered the calf and was about to pull the trigger. Hesitating, he whispered to Wetzel:

"If I fire they may run toward us."

"Nope, they'll run away," answered Wetzel.

Joe quickly covered the calf again and pulled the trigger. Bellowing, the big bull dashed off. The herd swung around toward the west and soon were galloping off with a lumbering roar. The shaggy humps bobbed up and down like waves on a storm-tossed sea.

Going forward, Wetzel and Joe found the calf lying dead in the grass.

"Might have did better," said the hunter. "Went a leetle too fer back, but mebbe the calf stepped as you shot."

CHAPTER FIFTEEN

ON GIRTY'S TRAIL

The days passed swiftly, each one bringing Joe a keener delight. Within a month he was as good a woodsman as many pioneers who had spent years on the border. He had the advantage of a teacher whose woodcraft was superlative, and besides he was naturally quick to learn, centering all his interest on forest lore.

Still he lacked, as did nearly all white men, the forest instinct which made the Indian as much at home in the woods as in his tepee. This Wetzel had developed to a high degree. Years of training and relentless hunting of Indians had given him a knowledge of the wilds that appalled his red-skinned foes.

Joe practiced trailing deer and other game until he was as unfailing as a hound. Then he began to perfect the art of following a human being through the forest. For this, he had to use Wetzel's tracks. On soft or marshy ground, which Wetzel avoided where he could, he left a faint trail, but on a hard surface he might as well not have gone over the ground at all, for all the traces he left.

Joe's persistence served him well. He hung on, and the more he failed the harder he tried. Often he would slip out of the cave after Wetzel had gone and try to find which way he had taken.

He was always up to see the sun rise red over the eastern hills and chase the white mist from the valleys. Many hours he idled away, lying on his back, his eyes on the distant hills where the cloud shadows swept across with slow, majestic movements.

If Wetzel and Joe were far distant from the cave, as they often were, they made camp in the open woods, and it was here that Joe was the most content. The twilight shades around the campfire, the cheery glow of red embers, and the sweet smell of wood smoke all bore a powerful appeal for the boy.

The hunter would broil a venison steak or a partridge on the coals. Then they would talk and Wetzel would smoke as the darkness deepened. The stillness of the early evening always gave Joe a feeling of awe.

"Do you ever *feel* this stillness?" he asked Wetzel once as they sat near their flickering fire.

The hunter puffed at his pipe. "I've scalped redskins every hour in the day, 'cept twilight," he finally said.

Joe was satisfied. The hour which took Wetzel from his stern pursuit must be a bewitching one.

The next day the hunter told Joe they would go across country to seek new game fields. Accordingly they set out and tramped until evening. They came to a beautiful rolling country, watered by many springs and streams.

Joe's eagerness was aroused, for Wetzel had told him that this was a country much traveled by Indians, especially runners and hunting parties going north and south. A buffalo road ran through the center of the tract, and since the buffalo always picked out the straightest, lowest, and driest path from one range to another the Indians followed these first pathfinders.

They made camp on the bank of a stream that night, and as Joe watched the hunter build a hidden campfire, he peered furtively around, half expecting to see dark forms skulking through the forest. Wetzel stripped pieces of bark from fallen trees and built a little hut over his firewood, arranging the covering so that not a ray of light escaped. When the flames had subsided and the wood had burned down to a glowing bed of red he threw aside the bark and broiled the strips of venison they had brought with them.

They rested on a bed of boughs which they had cut and arranged alongside a huge log. For hours Joe lay awake. He could not get to sleep. Finally he turned over. The slight noise instantly awakened Wetzel, who lifted his head and listened intently.

Then with the single word, "Sleep," he lay back again. Joe forced himself to be quiet, relaxed all his muscles, and soon was slumbering.

On the next day Wetzel went out to look over the hunting prospects. He returned about noon.

"I seen Injun sign," he said. "No tellin' how soon we may run ag'in' the sneaks. We can't hunt here—like as not thar's Hurons and Delawares skulkin' around. I think I'd best take you back to the village."

"If you were alone what would you do?"

"I calkilate I'd hunt fer some red-skinned game."

Joe's heart beat hard. "I won't go back to the village," he declared.

The hunter stood leaning on his rifle and made no response.

"I won't go," Joe repeated earnestly. "Let me stay with you. If at any time I hinder you or can't keep the pace then leave me to shift for myself, but don't make me go unless I weaken."

Suddenly Wetzel took Joe's hand and gave it a viselike squeeze.

"Wal, lad, stay," he said with his rare smile. "We'll hang round these diggin's a few days. First off we'll take in the lay of the land. You go downstream a ways and scout round some, while I go up and then circle down. Move slow, now, and don't miss nothin'."

Joe followed the stream a mile or more. He kept close in the shade of willows and waited and watched before walking across an open glade. He listened carefully but heard no unfamiliar sounds. He studied the sand along the stream and the leaves and moss

under the trees. When he had been separated from
Wetzel for two or three hours he decided he would
return to camp. Starting out, he ran across a well-
beaten path winding through the forest. He bent
over the worn grass to study it closely.

Crack!

The loud report of a rifle rang out. Joe felt the
zip of the bullet as it fanned his cheek. He leaped
to gain the shelter of a tree, then peeped out. He
saw the dark form of an Indian melt into the foliage
a hundred yards down the path. Joe expected to see
other Indians and hear more shots, but nothing
happened.

Joe watched the place where the Indian had disappeared and presently saw a dark hand, then a naked
elbow, and finally the ramrod of a rifle. The brave
was reloading. Soon a rifle barrel protruded from
behind the tree.

Joe screened his body as best he could. The tree
was small but it partly protected him. He tried to
think of a plan by which he could outwit his enemy.
The Indian was behind a large oak with a low limb
over which he could fire without exposing much of
himself.

Crack!

The bullet crumbled the bark close to Joe's face.
He yelled loudly, floundered to his knees, and fell
into the path, where he lay quiet.

The redskin gave an exultant shout. Seeing that

the fallen figure remained quite motionless, he stepped forward, drawing his knife as he came.

Suddenly Joe sat up, raising his rifle as he did so, and fired point-blank at the Indian.

He missed.

The Indian stopped open-mouthed when he saw Joe thus seemingly come back to life. Then, realizing that Joe had wasted his shot, he bounded forward, brandishing his knife.

Joe jumped to his feet, swinging his rifle above his head. When the savage was so near that Joe could plainly see every feature of his hate-twisted face, a peculiar whistling noise sounded over the boy's shoulder. It was accompanied by a clear, ringing rifle shot.

The Indian stopped in his tracks, as if he had run into an invisible wall which barred the way. Clutching at his breast, he uttered a strangling cry and sank to the grass.

Joe ran forward to bend over the savage. He was a slender, good-looking young brave. He held one hand tightly over the wound in his chest while blood trickled between the fingers to run down his side and stain the grass. He looked steadily up at Joe, with no yielding in the dark eyes, nothing but a challenging hatred. Then the eyes glazed and the clutching fingers relaxed.

Joe shrank back from this violent death of a human being. His heart beat fast and his hands trembled. He felt a strange coldness in all his being.

Then he felt, rather than heard, someone approaching and turned to see Wetzel coming down the path.

"A lone Shawnee runner," said the hunter, peering down at the dead Indian. "Tryin' to win his eagle plumes. I seen you both from the hillside."

"You did!" exclaimed Joe. "That was lucky for me. I tried the trick you taught me, but I was so eager I missed."

"You hadn't no call fer hurry. You worked the trick clever, and still missed him when there was plenty of time. I had to shoot over yer shoulder or I'd have plugged him sooner."

"Where were you?" asked Joe.

"Up thar by that bit of sumach." Wetzel pointed to an open ridge on a hillside at least a hundred and fifty yards distant.

Joe wondered for a moment which of the two bullets—Wetzel's or the Indian's—had passed closer to him.

"Come," said the hunter after he had scalped the brave.

"What's to be done with him?" Joe asked, indicating the fallen Indian.

"Jest let him lay."

They returned to camp, where the hunter set about repairing their temporary shelter, for there were clouds in the sky that threatened a storm. Joe cut up some buffalo meat and then went down to the brook for a gourd of water. He came back hurriedly.

"Come quick," he said to Wetzel. "I've seen something which may mean a great deal."

He led the way back to the brookside. "Look." He pointed at the water.

Here the stream was about two feet deep, perhaps twenty feet wide, and had just a noticeable current. Shortly before, it had been as clear as a bright summer sky. Now it was tinged with yellow clouds that floated slowly downstream, each one enlarging and becoming fainter as it spread into the clear water. Grains of sand glided along with the current. Little pieces of bark floated on the surface.

"Deer wouldn't roil the water like that. What does it mean?" asked Joe.

"Injuns, and not fer away."

Wetzel returned to the shelter and tore it down. Then he bent the branch of a beech tree low over the place. He pulled another branch over the remains of the campfire.

This done, the hunter grasped Joe's hand and led him up the knoll. Making his way behind a thickly foliaged tree which had been uprooted, he selected a position where, while hidden themselves, they could watch the creek.

Hardly had Wetzel warned Joe to lie perfectly still when from a short distance up the stream came the sound of splashing water. Still, nothing could be seen above the open glade, as in that direction willows lined the creek in dense thickets. The noise grew louder.

Suddenly Joe sensed a tightening of all the muscles in the powerful body that lay beside his. It was like that which might pass through the body of a tiger about to spring upon its prey. The boy shuddered as a cold chill gripped his own body.

After a few more moments of breathless suspense, a tall Indian warrior glided into the open space along the creek. He was knee-deep in the water, wading with slow, cautious steps.

His gaudy costume seemed familiar to Joe. He carried his rifle low, and as he passed slowly along with apparent distrust Joe thought he recognized that head, with the tangled black hair. Then, when he caught a better glimpse of the swarthy face, he could not help uttering a hoarse whisper:

"Girty! By—"

Wetzel's powerful arm forced him so hard against the log that he could not complete his exclamation, but he could still see. Girty had not heard the stifled cry. He continued his slow wading, and soon his tall form passed out of sight.

Another savage appeared in the open space, and then another. Close between them walked a white man, with hands bound behind him. Prisoner and guards disappeared downstream behind the willows.

The splashing sounds continued, grew louder than

before. A warrior came into view, then another, and a third. They walked close together. They were wading by a raft made of several logs, upon which lay two human figures.

Joe was watching the lithe forms of the Indians so intently that he barely got a glimpse of their floating prize. Then, bringing up the rear, he saw the Shawnee chieftain, Silvertip.

When Silvertip, too, passed out of sight behind the willows, Joe was trembling all over. He turned eagerly to Wetzel.

The hunter's face was stern and somber. His dark eyes glittered with a deadly light. "Three white captives, two of 'em women," he muttered.

"Were those women on the raft?" queried Joe, and when Wetzel nodded he continued: "A white man and two women, six warriors, Silvertip, and that renegade Jim Girty!"

Wetzel did not bother to reply to this. In a few words he directed Joe to cut up as much of the buffalo meat as they could stow in their pockets. Then he turned into the woods and, with Joe following, walked along rapidly, stopping now and then for a brief instant. Soon they emerged from the forest into more open country.

They faced a wide plain bordered on the right by a long, winding strip of bright green willows which marked the course of the stream. On the edge of this plain Wetzel broke into a run. He kept this pace

Two Women Lay on the Raft

for some distance, then stopped to listen intently as he glanced sharply on all sides. Then he was off again.

Halfway across the plain Joe's wind began to fail and his breathing became labored, but he kept close to the hunter's heels. Once he looked back at the wide expanse of waving grass. They had covered perhaps four miles and were nearing the other side of the plain. He felt as if his head were about to burst. There was a sharp pain in his side and there seemed to be a blood-red film before his eyes. Utterly exhausted, he fell to the ground.

When he had recovered his breath he got up. They had crossed the plain and were in a grove of beeches. In front of him was a swift stream which was divided by the rocky head of a point of land. The two branches of the creek took almost opposite courses.

Joe was drenched with perspiration. He glanced at Wetzel. The man's broad breast rose and fell a little faster, but that was the only evidence of the grueling four-mile run.

"They've got ahead of us, but which crick did they take?" Wetzel said, as if to himself.

"How do you know they've passed?" Joe queried.

Wetzel pointed into the bushes. Looking into the thicket, Joe found dead leaves, sticks, and litter thrown aside, exposing a long, hollowed place on the ground. Little furrows in the hollowed place, holes and winding passages showed where grubs and crickets had made their homes. The insects were now running around wildly.

"What was here—a log?"

"A twenty-foot canoe was hid under that stuff. The Injuns have jest set out on one of these streams."

"How can we tell which one?"

"Mebbe we can't, but we'll try. Grab a few of them bugs, go below that rocky point, and crawl close to the bank so you can jest peep over. Be keerful not to show the tip of your head and don't knock nothin' off'n the bank so's it'll drop into the water. Watch fer trout. Look everywhere, and drop in a bug now and then. I'll do the same fer the other stream. Then we'll come back here and talk over what the fish has to say about the Injuns."

Joe walked downstream a few paces and, dropping on his knees, crawled carefully to the edge of the bank. He was directly over a pool with a narrow shoal running out from the opposite bank. The water was so clear that he could see the pebbly bottom, except for a dark hole near the bend in the shore close by.

He flipped in one of the bugs. A shiny fish flared up from the depths of the deep hole and disappeared with the cricket, but it was a bass, not a trout. He tried again to coax one to the surface. This time the cricket swam across the stream to safety.

When his eyes were thoroughly accustomed to the clear water, with its deceiving lights and shadows,

Joe saw a fish lying snug by the side of a stone. He crawled to a better position farther down the stream and peered again through the weeds. Sure enough, it was a trout.

Joe tossed out a big cricket which landed on the water just above the fish. The trout did not move. He tried again, with no better success. The fish would not rise. Then Joe returned to the point where he had left Wetzel.

"Couldn't see nothin' over thar," said the waiting hunter. "You see any?"

"One, and a big fellow."

"Did he see you?"

"No."

"Did he rise to a bug?"

"No, he didn't, but maybe he wasn't hungry." Joe could not understand what Wetzel was getting at.

"Tell me exactly what he did."

"That's the trouble, he didn't do anything," said Joe. "He just lay, stiff-like, by a stone. He never batted an eye, but his side fins quivered like an aspen leaf."

"Them side fins tell us the story," said Wetzel positively. "Girty and his redskins has took this branch. The other leads to the Huron towns. Girty's got a place near the Delaware camp some'r's."

Joe gazed at Wetzel in silent admiration. To think that the hunter could read a story from the action of a fish!

"Here's where they got in the canoe. One more look, and then we're off."

Wetzel strode up and down the sandy beach, examined the willows, and studied the sand. Suddenly he bent over and picked up an object from the water's edge. His sharp eyes had caught the glint of a small ivory or bone buckle with a piece broken out. He showed it to Joe.

"By heavens, Wetzel, that's a buckle off Nell Wells's shoe! I've seen it too many times to be mistaken."

"I was afeered Girty had your friends, the two sisters, and yer brother, too."

"Come on! Let's kill the fiend!" said Joe, his lips white.

"I calkilate they're a mile or so downstream, makin' camp fer the night. I know the place they'd stop. Thar's a fine spring. Look—d'ye see them crows flyin' round the big oak with the bleached top? Hear 'em cawin'? They're makin' that fuss 'cause they see Injuns."

"Well?" Joe demanded impatiently.

"It'll be moonlight a while arter midnight. We'll lay low and wait, and then—" Wetzel's teeth came together with a sharp click, like that of a steel trap.

Joe said no more, but followed the hunter into the woods. Stopping near a fallen tree, Wetzel raked up a bundle of leaves and spread them on the ground. Then he cut a few spreading branches from a beech and leaned them against a log. Telling Joe to crawl in before him, he took one last look around and then made his way under the shelter.

It was still daylight, which seemed a strange time to do a thing like this. Joe thought it could not be to sleep, but simply to wait—wait for the long hours to pass. So he was amazed when, by the time twilight had passed, Wetzel was asleep. Joe had expected that they would rush to a combat with the foe—but no, this man, with his keen forest wisdom, knew when to creep up on the enemy. He bided that time, and while he waited he slept.

Joe was unable to keep his own eyes closed. Through the gaps in the branches he saw the stars come out one by one. The moments dragged. He heard a whippoorwill call, lonely and dismal. An owl hooted. A stealthy-footed animal ran along the log, sniffed at the boughs, and scurried away over the dry leaves.

By and by the dead silence of night fell over all. Still Joe lay wide awake, listening. His heart seemed on fire. He would rescue Nell—kill that hawk-nosed renegade—fight Silvertip to the death!

CHAPTER SIXTEEN

THE FIGHT AT THE SPRING

When the waning moon rose high enough to shed a pale light over forest and field, two dark figures, moving silently from the shadows of the trees, crossed the moonlit patches of ground, out to the open plain where silver mists hung low over the grass. Then, like specters, gliding swiftly with noiseless tread, the two figures vanished, swallowed by the long grass.

The plain, deserted once again, became unutterably lonely. There was no stir, no sound, no life—nothing but the wide expanse bathed in a sad, gray light.

The moon shone steadily. Its silver radiance mellowed, paling the stars.

Slowly the night hours wore away.

On the other side of the plain, where the bordering forest loomed dark and forbidding, the tall grasses parted. A dark form showed. Slowly it sank, and was lost. Once more the unwavering line of silver-crested grass tufts was unbroken.

Only the night breeze, wandering over the grass, might have told of two dark forms gliding softly and surely toward the forest. Only the moon and the pale stars had eyes to see these creeping figures.

On over the dark line where plain merged into forest they crawled. They slipped over the moss in single file, the leader clearing the path. Inch by inch they advanced. They did not rustle a leaf or snap a twig or shake a fern.

At last the top of a knoll was reached. The Avenger placed his hand on the shoulder of his follower. Then he glided away.

The one who was left behind raised his head to look into the open place. It was oval-shaped. A spring gemmed the center. An Indian guard stood statue-like against a stone. Other savages lay in a row, their shaven heads shining. One of the sleeping forms was bedecked with feathers and frills. Near him was an Indian blanket, from which two faces gleamed white in the moonlight.

The watcher trembled at the sight of those two faces. He must wait while long moments passed. He must wait for the Avenger to creep up, silently kill the guard, and release the prisoners without awakening the other savages. If that plan failed, he was to rush into the glade, and in the excitement make off with at least one of the captives.

He lay there, waiting, listening, worked up to a terrific pitch of fierce passion. Every nerve was alert, every tendon strung, every muscle strained, ready for the leap.

A strange feeling of horror suddenly swept over

the watching man. His hair stood straight up and a chill stole over him. He did not know whether it was the climax of the long night's excitement or thought of the bloody struggle soon to come.

Fighting back the numbing sense of horror, he fastened his gaze on the guard. The Indian's posture was the same as before but now it seemed to show a kind of strained attention. Somehow, the wary redskin had sensed danger.

A faint moan breathed low above the sound of gently splashing water, somewhere beyond the glade.

"*Woo-o-oo—*"

The guard's figure stiffened and became rigidly erect.

The soft breeze sighed in the treetops. Louder then, with a deep wail, a moan arose out of the dark gray shadows, swelled thrillingly on the still air, and died away mournfully.

"*Um-m-mmwoo-o-oo!*"

The form of the sentinel melted into the shadows. He was gone like a phantom.

Another Indian rose quickly and glanced furtively around the glade. He bent over a comrade and shook him. Instantly the second Indian was on his feet.

Then an object shot out of the thicket near them and hurled both warriors to the earth. A moonbeam glinted upon something bright. It flashed again, in a swift, sweeping circle. A short, choking yell aroused the other savages. They sprang up, alarmed and confused.

The shadow-form darted among them with unbelievable rapidity. Dull blows, the click of steel, angry shouts, yells of agony, and threshing sounds mingled together on the night air.

The battle ceased as suddenly as it had begun. Warriors lay still on the grass; others writhed in agony. For an instant a fleeting shadow crossed the open lane leading out of the glade, and then it vanished.

Three savages had leaped to get their rifles. A blinding flash and loud report burst from the thicket. The foremost savage sank to the ground. The others were faced by a giant shadow swinging a rifle. The watcher on the knoll had entered the glade, and now stood before the stacked rifles and swung his heavy gun.

One Indian went down before that deadly club, but rose again. The others backed away from this threatening figure, circled around it.

More savages joined those who ducked and dodged before their desperate foe. They closed in on him— and were beaten back. One threw a glittering knife, another a tomahawk which struck sparks from the flailing rifle.

He held them at bay. As long as they had no firearms he was the master of them. With every sweep of his arms he brought the long rifle down and knocked a flint from the firelock of an enemy's weapon. Soon the Indians' guns were all useless. Then he began to edge away slowly, toward the opening where he had seen the fleeing form vanish.

Too late—the Indians glided now before him, now behind him. He was surrounded. Round and round he turned, the ever-circling rifle whirling in the savages' faces.

Opposite the lane leading from the glade, he changed his tactics. He plunged into the midst of them, laying about him ferociously. They fell before the sweep of his powerful arms, grappling his legs as they went down.

He flung off savage after savage, until at last he had cleared the path before him. Away he bounded.

As he left the glade the guard who had vanished at the moaning sound stepped from behind a tree and cast his tomahawk. It glittered and flashed after the fleeing figure.

Suddenly the moonlit path darkened in the runner's sight. He saw a million flashing stars and knew an instant of terrible pain. Then he sank slowly down, and all was darkness—

CHAPTER SEVENTEEN

WHISPERING WINDS

Joe awoke as from some fearful nightmare. Acute pain pulsed through his temples. A bloody mist hindered his sight. Binding pressure cramped his arms and legs.

The bright sun, which made the dewdrops glisten on the leaves, lighted a scene of tragedy. Near him lay an Indian whose sightless eyes were fixed in death. Beyond him lay four more savages, the strange position of their limbs showing that they too had been claimed by death.

Joe remembered it all now—the advance, the rush, the fight, all returned. Again he saw Wetzel's shadowy form darting like a demon into the whirl of conflict. His gaze swept over the glade, but saw nothing of the hunter.

Silvertip and another Indian were bathing a wound on Girty's forehead. The renegade groaned and writhed in pain. Near him lay Kate, her face white and her eyes closed. Jim sat crouched under a tree to which he was tied.

"Joe, are you badly hurt?" Jim asked, noticing that his brother had come to.

"No—I guess not," he managed to answer. "Poor Kate—is she—dead?"

"No. I think she fainted."

"Where is Nell?"

"Gone." Jim lowered his voice. "That whirlwind was Wetzel, wasn't it?"

"Yes—but how'd you know?"

"I was awake when it started. Something oppressed my mind, I couldn't sleep. I heard that wind moaning through the forest, and I thought my blood would freeze. Then I saw Silvertip disappear and the other two savages rise. Then something huge seemed to drop out of the sky right next to them, a bright thing flashed at them in the moonlight, and they yelled and dropped to the ground.

"It was when Wetzel plunged into the midst of the other Indians that I recognized him. He had something wrapped around his left arm—maybe it was his coat—and his right hand held a tomahawk. I saw him strike that big Indian lying there.

"He broke through the circle, swung Nell under his arm, slashed at my ropes as he passed by, and then was gone. Not until after you were struck, and Silvertip came up to me, did I realize that my bonds were cut. I was free to help, to fight—and I did not know it, fool that I am!"

"Well, I made enough of a mess of my part," groaned Joe. "Did the Indians know it was Wetzel?"

"I should think so! Didn't you hear them scream-

ing that French name? Only two of them died out-
right, I think. The others held on for most of the
night, and I sat here, tied and helpless, listening to
them groan and cry out that name. Deathwind—
they have named him well!"

"I guess he nearly killed Girty."

"Nearly, but not quite. The devil himself must
protect that renegade."

"Jim Girty is doomed," Joe whispered earnestly.
"He's as good as dead already. I've lived with Wetzel, and I *know*. I saw it in his eyes. I almost expect
him to jump out of these bushes any minute. If he
knows there are only three of them left, he'll be after
them, all right. Where's Girty taking you?"

"To the Delaware town— Hush! Girty's up."

The renegade staggered to an upright position,
leaning on the Shawnee's arm. There was a swollen,
gashed lump on his temple.

"Whar's the yeller-haired gal?" he demanded,
glaring around.

The Shawnee spoke to him briefly, and Girty
howled out his rage.

"I'll git her ag'in!" he roared. "And I'll keep her
when I do!"

"You'll never get her!" Joe called to him loudly.
"Wetzel will kill you first!"

The renegade turned his evil gaze in the direction of the boy. He spat.

"I'll see you finished at the stake, beggin' fer mercy," he croaked. "Then I'll feed ye t' the buzzards!"

"You'd better kill me now and then go sneaking to your hole like a hyena and stay there!" Joe taunted him. "Wetzel is on your trail—he's after you, Girty—he'll get you one of these days, and when he does—"

Girty's swarthy, evil face turned white with fear. He cringed for a moment, as though expecting the hunter to show up then and there, wielding his vengeful blade. He shook himself, as though casting off a fearful spell.

"I'll shet yer wind!" he yelped, catching up his tomahawk and making for Joe.

Silvertip interrupted, preventing the attack. He led Girty back to his seat, talking to him in a low, rapid voice.

"Silvertip, give me a tomahawk and let me fight him," Joe begged of the redskin.

"Paleface brave—like Injun chief," Silvertip answered with respect in his voice. "Paleface Shawnee's prisoner. No speak more."

"Oh, where's Nellie?" As the grief-stricken whisper caught Jim's ear he turned to see Kate's wide, questioning, anxious eyes fixed on him.

"Nell was rescued," he answered.

"Thank heaven!" murmured the girl.

"Come along," shouted Girty in his harsh voice. Grasping Kate's arm, he pulled her roughly to her feet. Then, picking up his rifle, he led her into the forest. Silvertip followed with Joe, and the remaining Indian guarded Jim.

The great council lodge of the Delawares rang with savage and fiery eloquence. Wingenund paced slowly before the orators, seeking their advice before deciding what was to be done with the missionary.

The Indians sat in a half circle around the lodge. The two prisoners, guarded by two brawny braves, stood in one corner, gazing with curiosity and not a little concern at this great array.

Jim knew some of the braves who were present, but most of those who spoke bitterly against the palefaces he had never seen at the Village of Peace. Two white men, both dressed in Indian garb, occupied a prominent place before Wingenund. The brothers saw a resemblance between one of these men and Jim Girty, and so concluded he was the famous renegade, Simon Girty. The other man was probably Elliott, the Tory. Jim Girty was not present. Upon nearing the camp, he had taken his captive, Kate, and disappeared with her into a ravine.

Shingiss, who had a reputation for being easy on prisoners, urged that the brothers should be initiated into the tribe. Several other chiefs seemed to favor this idea, though not as strongly as did Shingiss. Kotoxen argued that they should be put to death and the bloodthirsty Pipe insisted that they should be burned at the stake. Not one was for returning the missionary to the Christian Indians. Girty and Elliott were asked to speak, but they kept an ominous silence.

Wingenund strode back and forth before the council, his brow wrinkled in thought. Freedom or death for the captives would be decided by the wave of his hand. His expression did not give them the slightest inkling of what to expect.

"Wingenund has heard the Delaware wise men and warriors," he finally announced. "The White Indian does not open his lips, and his silence bodes evil for the palefaces. Pipe wants the blood of the white men; he demands the stake.

"Now Wingenund says to free the white father who harms no Indian. Wingenund hears no evil in the sound of his voice. But the white father's brother should die—kill the companion of Deathwind!"

A murmur ran around the circle when the great chieftain mentioned the dreaded name.

"The white father is free," continued Wingenund. "Let one of my runners conduct him to the Village of Peace."

A brave entered and touched Jim on the shoulder. Jim shook his head and pointed to Joe. The runner then touched Joe.

"No, no, I'm not the missionary," cried Joe and stared at his brother aghast. "Jim, have you lost your senses?"

Shaking his head sadly, Jim turned to Wingenund

and told him in the Indian tongue that his brother
was the missionary and was trying to sacrifice himself, taking this opportunity to practice the Christianity that he had been teaching.

"The white father is brave, but he is known,"
Wingenund said, pointing to the door of his lodge.
"Let him go back to his Christian Indians."

The Indian runner cut Joe's bonds and tried to
lead him from the lodge. Pushing the runner aside,
Joe soon exhausted the few Indian words he knew
in a vain attempt to convince them that he was not
the missionary. He even begged Girty to speak for
him, and when the renegade sat stolidly silent Joe's
rage burst out:

"Curse you all for a lot of ignorant redskins! I am
not a missionary—I am Deathwind's friend! I killed
a Delaware—I was the companion of *Le Vent de la
Mort!*"

The passionate insistence with which Joe spoke
won the interest and respect, if not belief, of the as-
sembled Indians. Here were two brothers, each willing to go to the stake and suffer awful agony for the
sake of the other. It was the sort of thing an Indian
might do. They shook their heads admiringly.

"Let the white father stand forth!" called Wingenund sternly, in an attempt to settle it.

A hundred dark eyes turned on the two prisoners. Except that one wore a buckskin coat and the
other a linsey one, there was no difference in the

pair, each one firm in his refusal to step forward. The strong figures were the same, the set faces alike, the resolute gray eyes identical.

Suddenly it came to Wingenund how he could decide. "Let my daughter come," he ordered.

A slight figure soon entered the lodge. It was Whispering Winds. Her face glowed as she listened to her father.

"Wingenund's daughter has her mother's eyes, that were as beautiful as a doe's, as keen as a hawk's, as farseeing as an eagle's. Let the Delaware maiden show her blood—let her point out the white father."

Shyly but without hesitation Whispering Winds laid her hand on Jim's arm.

"Missionary, be gone," rolled out the chief. "And thank the daughter of Wingenund for your life, not the God of your Christians!"

He waved his hand to the runner and the brave grasped Jim's arm.

"Good-by, Joe," Jim said brokenly.

"Good-by, old fellow," came the answer.

They took one last long look into each other's eyes and parted.

"Let the Shawnee chief paint his prisoner black," commanded Wingenund.

When the missionary had left the lodge with the runner, Whispering Winds had smiled, for she had saved the one whom she loved to hear speak. But now the dread command that followed paled her cheek. Black paint meant a hideous death. She looked at this man, so like the white father. Her piteous gaze tried to turn from that white face, but the cold, steely eyes fascinated her.

She had saved one of them, only to be the other's doom! Now she resolved to save him, too.

As she stepped toward the captive and took his hand, she felt her whole body glow with conscious pride in her power. It was the knowledge that still she could save.

When she kissed his hand and knelt before him, she claimed the unquestionable right of an Indian maiden. She asked what no Indian dared refuse a chief's daughter—she took the paleface for her husband.

Her action was followed by a stunned silence. She remained kneeling as Wingenund resumed his slow march to and fro. Silvertip retired to one corner with a gloomy face. The others bowed their heads, some humble, a few half-defiant in their hearts but not daring to show it openly.

Once more the chieftain's deep voice rang out. An old Indian, wrinkled and worn but wearing a strange and weird costume, entered the lodge and waved a slender wandlike stick. He mumbled some strange words and departed, chanting a long song.

Whispering Winds rose, a soft smile playing over her face. Still holding Joe's hand, she led him out of the lodge, through long rows of silent Indians, and down a lane bordered by tepees, he following like one in a dream.

She finally halted before a large, imposing-looking lodge and indicated that he should enter. Still silent, he obeyed.

The girl turned to Joe. Her lips quivered and she caught her breath.

"Whispering Winds—save paleface," she said in a low, tremulous voice. "Fear father. Fear tell Wingenund—she Christian."

Indian summer unfolded its golden, dreamy haze over the Delaware village. The forests blazed with autumn colors; the meadows bloomed in rich productiveness. All day there hung low in the valleys a purple smoke which changed into a white mist as the cool evening shades crept out of the woodland.

For Joe, these were days of enchantment. He was a willing captive now, for his wild heart had found its mate. He surrendered himself to love for his Indian bride.

One day she asked Joe to teach her more about truth and God. "Whispering Winds wants to go to the Christians," she said, "but she fears her father. Wingenund would burn the Village of Peace. But be patient, my husband. Whispering Winds will set you free and be free herself to go far with you toward the rising sun, where your people dwell. She will love your people and raise Christian children.

Or, if you will it, we shall live the Indian life, free as two eagles."

Although Joe was happy with the beautiful Indian girl he did not forget that Kate was still in the power of the renegade and that he must rescue her. He knew that Girty was keeping the girl somewhere near the Delaware camp, and he determined to find the place. He turned over in his mind plans of all kinds.

Meanwhile, he mingled freely with the Indians. His friendly personality, combined with his great strength and physical prowess, soon made him well liked. He even got on good terms with Pipe, whose sense of humor he tickled with all the practical jokes that he played on the younger braves, especially the ones who had in the past been suitors for the hand of Whispering Winds. Of course Joe's pranks did not sit well with them, but they feared the muscular paleface, and the ridicule of the tribe even more, so they pretended an unconcern they did not feel.

Joe's idea was to convince the savages that he was thoroughly happy in his new life. So he was, but it would suit him even better to be free. He succeeded in misleading the Indians. At first he was closely watched, but after a while the vigilance relaxed, finally to cease altogether.

This last fact was no doubt owing largely to a great excitement that had suddenly taken hold of the Delawares. Council after council was held in the big lodge. The camp was visited by one runner after another. Something important was brewing, though Joe could not learn what it all meant.

Even Whispering Winds lost her lightness of spirit and became sad. When he asked her the reason she would not tell him. Then she surprised him by indicating that she was eager for the two of them to flee immediately.

Simon Girty and Elliott, together with several other renegades whom Joe did not know, were much in evidence and their presence seemed to add to the unrest of the camp. They were busy all day and far into the night. Joe often heard Girty's hoarse voice lifted in the council lodge. Pipe was thundering constantly for war, although Joe could not learn against whom. Elliott's smooth, oily speech urged the Indians to vengeance—but again, Joe could not guess on whom.

On the third day of the councils a horseman stopped before the lodge of Whispering Winds and called to her. Stepping to the entrance, Joe saw a white man whose keen, handsome face seemed familiar, though he was a stranger.

"A word with you," said the man to Joe in a curt voice, that of one used to power and authority.

"As many as you like," Joe responded. "Who are you?"

"I am Isaac Zane. Are you Wetzel's companion, or the renegade, Deering?" the other demanded.

"I'm not a renegade any more than you are," Joe retorted, for he remembered that this was the brother of Colonel Zane who lived with another Indian tribe. "I was rescued by this Indian girl, and I am now her husband."

"Good! I'm glad to meet you," Zane replied instantly, his manner changing. He extended his hand. "I had to be sure. I'm on my way to the Wyandot town. I've been to Fort Henry, where my brother told me of you and the missionaries. When I got here I heard your story from Simon Girty. You ought to get away from here if you can. I'd take you to the Huron village if I dared, but it's impossible. But leave here, get out—while you have a chance!"

"Zane, I thank you. I've suspected something was wrong—tell me what it is."

"Couldn't be worse," whispered Zane, glancing around cautiously. "Girty and Elliott, with this man Deering, are becoming afraid of the influence of Christianity on the Indians. They're plotting against the Village of Peace. Tarhe, the Huron chief, has been asked to join in a concerted move against the white man's religion. The renegades seem to be fuming over the converted Indians more than the missionaries. They want to break the missionaries' hold by killing the Christian Indians. Pipe is wild for blood. It looks bad—*bad!*"

"What should I do?"

"Cut out for yourself. Get away with a gun, if you

can. Take the creek below, follow it down to the Ohio, then make east for Fort Henry."

"But Jim Girty's got a white girl hidden around here somewhere, and I want to rescue her."

"Don't throw your life away! Girty's probably sold the girl as a slave to some Indian chief or other by this time."

"Well, I won't leave without trying. And there's my wife, this Indian girl who saved me. She's a Christian, Zane, and she wants to go with me. I can't leave her."

"I'm warning you, that's all. I admit that if I were you, I'd never leave without a try to find the white girl, nor would I forsake my Indian bride. Pick out a favorable time and make your attempt. Ask your wife to show you where Girty is—she probably knows but has been afraid to tell you, for fear of Girty. Get your dog and horse from the Shawnee. That's a fine horse, and he can carry you both to safety. Take him away from Silvertip."

"How?"

"Go right up and demand your horse and dog. Most of these Delawares are honest, and they respect anyone who sticks up for his rights. They don't like the Shawnee, anyhow. If Silvertip refuses to give you the horse, grab him and beat him good—you're big enough to do it. The Delawares will be tickled. Do it openly, and no one will interfere."

"By heaven, I'll give him a drubbing!" cried Joe.

"I must go now. I'll send a Wyandot runner to your brother at the village, so they'll be warned. Good-by and good luck—may we meet again."

Joe watched Zane ride swiftly down the lane and disappear in the shrubbery. He went inside and informed Whispering Winds that he had learned the reason for the councils, that he had decided to get away, and that she must locate Girty's hiding-place.

She told him that she knew the direction from which Girty always returned to the village and that she was confident she could find his hide-out. Then she suggested a plan which seemed to Joe a good one. After he had got his horse she would ride around the village, then off into the woods, where she would leave the horse and return to say he had run away from her. As was their custom of an afternoon, they would walk leisurely along the brook and get away unobserved, find the horse, rescue Kate, if possible, and travel east with all speed.

Joe left the lodge at once. Luck favored him at the outset, for he met Silvertip in front of the council lodge. The Shawnee was leading Lance, and the dog was following at his heels.

In full view of a crowd of Indians who were waiting for the council to begin, Joe planted himself in front of the Shawnee, barring the way.

"Silvertip has the paleface's horse and dog," he said in a loud voice.

The Shawnee stared haughtily and the surround-

Joe Barred Silvertip's Way

ing Delawares sauntered closer. They all knew how
Silvertip had got the animals, and they awaited the
outcome of Joe's challenge with interest.

"Paleface heap liar," growled the Shawnee. His
hand dropped, apparently carelessly, to the haft of
his tomahawk.

Joe swung his long arm and his big fist caught Silvertip on the jaw, sending him sprawling to the
ground. With a shrill yell he drew his weapon and
tried to rise.

One kick sent the tomahawk spinning, a second
dumped the Shawnee back on the ground. Blind
with rage now, Silvertip leaped to his feet and tried
to grapple with his antagonist.

Shifty and elusive, Joe dodged around the savage.
One, two, three sharp blows staggered Silvertip and
then, with the Indian off balance, a powerful one
felled him, battered and bloody, on the grass. The
Delawares looked down at the vanquished Shawnee,
grunting in approval.

With Lance prancing proudly and Mose leaping
lovingly beside him, Joe walked back to his lodge.
Whispering Winds ran to meet him, her face joyful.

She told Joe that an important council was to be
held that afternoon. It would be well for them to
make their getaway immediately after the conven-
ing of the chiefs. Accordingly, she mounted Lance
and rode up and down the camp. She let everyone in
the place see her clinging to the back of the black

stallion. Then she rode him out along the creek. When she returned afoot an hour later, with her hair flying and clothing mussed, no one paid particular attention to her.

That afternoon, with Mose running before them, they got clear of the camp and into the woods. Whispering Winds led the way east. When they climbed to the top of a rocky ridge she pointed down into a thicket before them, saying that somewhere in this dense hollow was Girty's hut.

Joe hesitated about taking Mose. He wanted the dog, but in case he had to run it would be necessary for Whispering Winds to find his trail, and for this he left the dog with her.

He started down the ridge and soon, over some gray boulders, he saw the thatched roof of a hut. Picking out the best path over rough stones and through brambles, he kept always under cover.

Soon he reached level ground. A dense laurel thicket hid the cabin, but he knew about where it lay. Throwing himself flat on the ground, he wormed his way through the thicket. Finally the rear of the cabin stood before him.

It was made of logs, roughly hewn and as roughly thrown together. In several places clay had fallen from the chinks between the timbers, leaving small holes. Slipping closer to the hut, he raised his head and looked through one of the cracks.

CHAPTER EIGHTEEN

KNIFE AND TOMAHAWK

The sight which Joe saw horrified him into helpless inaction for several moments. Stunned, he gazed up through the open space in the leaves, trying to get himself under control, to still the fury which blazed within him. The soft blue of the sky, the fleecy clouds drifting, the gently fluttering leaves—all assured him he was wide awake. Again, then, he peeped through the hole.

Girty lay on a buffalo robe near a barred door. Beyond him sat Kate, huddled in a corner of the cabin. A long buckskin thong was knotted about her waist and tied to a log. Her hair was matted and tangled, and Joe could see bruises on her face and arms. Her head was bowed and she seemed to be weeping silently.

Joe clenched his hands until the nails bit into the flesh of his palms. *Be calm, be cool,* he heard Wetzel's voice whispering to him—

Suddenly he rose to his feet and with a spring hurled his heavy frame against the door.

Crash! The door was wrenched from its fastenings. Girty leaped up with a startled yell, drawing his knife as he did so. He had no time to use it before Joe was on top of him. As the two went down Joe caught Girty's wrist with a grip that cracked the bones. The knife fell and rolled away from the struggling men.

For perhaps a minute they tumbled about on the floor, locked in a crushing embrace. The renegade was as supple and slippery as an eel. Twice he wriggled out of Joe's grasp. Twice Joe pulled him down again, as a wolf would a deer. Finally he struck the renegade a heavy blow on the temple and his struggling became weaker.

With his knee on Girty's chest, Joe reached for the knife and swung it high. But just before he plunged it downward it was knocked from his hand. He jumped up to find himself facing Silvertip. The Shawnee held a tomahawk with which he had struck the knife from Joe's grasp.

Instantly Joe saw that Girty was helpless for the moment, that Silvertip was confident of revenge, and that he must follow Wetzel's advice: "Act like lightnin'."

Leaping past Silvertip, he bent and seized a wooden bar which lay on the floor. With this as a weapon, he rushed at the Indian. There began a duel in which the savage's quickness and cunning matched the white man's strength and fury.

Silvertip dodged most of the vicious swings Joe aimed at him. Others he parried. Nimble as a cat, he avoided every rush, his dark eyes watching for an opening.

At last, catching the bar on his tomahawk, he broke the force of the blow and suddenly, dropping to the ground, he grappled Joe's legs. Long before this, he had drawn his knife with his free hand, and now he used it, plunging the blade into Joe's side.

Withstanding the sharp pain as they fell together, Joe caught hold of Silvertip's wrist. Exerting all his power, he wrenched the Indian's arm so that the bones cracked.

Crippled though he was, Silvertip made a supreme effort, struggling desperately to twist away from Joe, but he was held in a grip of remorseless fury. Joe caught up the knife, which had fallen from Silvertip's crippled hand, and thrust it deep into the Indian's side.

Silvertip's muscles suddenly relaxed. Slowly his legs straightened. His arms dropped. His eyes lost their hate. They seemed to look far beyond, then to become fixed and unseeing.

Joe turned to see what Girty was doing. The renegade was gone. Then swiftly he released Kate and helped her to her feet. She seemed unable to understand what was happening, and Joe judged she was temporarily unbalanced by her grief and misery.

He started to leave the cabin, but realizing he was seriously wounded and thinking that he must not leave the place without weapons, he took the renegade's rifle from where it hung on some wall pegs.

As he led Kate forth, he was conscious of a queer lightness in his head but he felt no pain. He grew weaker and weaker as they made their way through the brush, and his head began to whirl, but he kept on. When they reached the top of the ridge he called aloud, and then plunged forward on his face. Dimly, as though from afar, he heard the whine of a dog.

When he regained his senses he was lying on a bed of ferns under a projecting rock. The gurgle of running water mingled with the songs of birds. Near him lay Mose and beyond him, sleeping, was Kate.

Finding he could move without difficulty, he put his hand on the spot where he had been stabbed and felt a soft compress. He decided that Whispering Winds had found them, made them as comfortable as possible, and then gone looking for food, or possibly back to the encampment.

As he lay there waiting for Whispering Winds to return, his thoughts were bitter. The odds were against their escape now. Girty would have the Delawares on their trail like a pack of hungry wolves. He had managed to free Kate from the man's evil clutches, but now she seemed to be doomed to be his slave again.

He had no fear of starvation, even if Whispering Winds failed to come back. He might lack the strength to use Girty's rifle, which lay near, but Mose could always catch a rabbit or woodchuck. What worried him most was pursuit. His trail from the cabin could be easily followed. He dared not start until his wound had had some time to heal. Perhaps he could persuade Whispering Winds to take Kate back to the Village of Peace and leave him there until help could come—

A low growl from Mose broke into his reflections. The dog had raised his head and was sniffing the air suspiciously. Joe heard a slight rustling, and then was overjoyed to see Whispering Winds. She came swiftly, and knelt beside him, murmuring words of love.

"Where have you been?" he asked her.

She told him that the dog had led her to him and Kate two evenings before. He was unconscious, and Kate did not seem to know what was going on. She had washed and bandaged his wound and remained with them all that night. The next day he was out of his head with fever and she decided to risk returning to the village. She could tell them he had left her. Then she could make her way back to him, bringing food and healing herbs.

Girty had returned to the camp. He was bruised and battered and in a white heat of fury. Going to Wingenund, he openly accused the girl of aiding her paleface lover to escape. Wingenund called his daughter to him and questioned her. She confessed all to him.

"Why is the daughter of Wingenund a traitor to

her tribe?" he demanded.

"Whispering Winds is a Christian," she told him.

Wingenund dismissed Girty and sent his braves from the lodge. When they were alone the chief told her that she was to leave his lodge and never return.

"Whispering Winds is free," were his last words.

Tears shone in the Indian girl's eyes when she told Joe her story.

"I am free," she said. "When strength returns so that you may travel we shall go to the white village. There we will live together."

"We have no one to fear then?" asked Joe.

"No red man, now that the Shawnee is dead."

"But Girty may follow us—and he would fear to come alone."

Two long days followed, during which the three lay quietly in hiding. On the morning of the third day Joe felt he might risk the start for the Village of Peace. Whispering Winds led Lance, upon whom both Joe and Kate rode. The white girl seemed to be recovering her mental balance slowly, though she still spoke seldom.

The sun was just gilding the horizon when they came out of the woods into a wide plain. Along the edge of the forest the ground was level and the going was easy. Several times during the morning Joe dismounted to rest. Kate appeared not to grow tired, even managing a wan smile once or twice. They covered several miles.

Then, as they were nearing a knoll covered with trees and shrubbery, Whispering Winds looked back and noticed that Joe's wound had opened and was bleeding again. She said they must stop here and stay until he was stronger.

Joe agreed that this was wise. They should be safe now, several miles from the Delaware camp. He got down and sat on a log while Whispering Winds helped Kate to dismount. Then the Indian girl searched for a good place in which to build a temporary shelter.

Joe's gaze was arrested by a tree with a huge knot near the ground. He was sure he had seen it before. He looked around on all sides. Just behind him was an opening in the clump of trees. In the opening was a high stone covered with moss and lichens. Above it a beech tree spread its long, graceful branches.

He thrilled with remembrance. This was the place where Wetzel had killed the Indians and rescued Nell.

CHAPTER NINETEEN

One evening a week or more after the disappearance of Jim and the girls, Young and Edwards, the missionaries, sat on the cabin steps, downheartedly gazing at the forest scenery.

"Dave, I tell you your theory about seeing them again is absurd," said Young. "I'll never forget the way that wretch, Girty, spoke to Nell. I'm sure he means to make her his slave. Why he let me go and took Jim I can't understand, unless the Shawnee had something to do with it. I never wished before that I was a hunter, but if I only was I'd go after that Girty myself! He doesn't deserve to live."

"George," answered Edwards, "I feel much the same way. It's on my mind constantly. I can't preach and I can't work."

"Neither can I. But, Dave, we still have our duty. To endure—that is our life."

"But this border life is so cruel!"

"Yes, it is cruel—and we have chosen to spend our lives here, in the middle of this unending strife, ·lacking the ordinary pleasures of life, so that a few dozen savages may be converted to the true faith."

"You speak truly, George. It is enough—though it is hard to give up those you love."

At this point Heckewelder and Mr. Wells came out of the adjoining cabin. Heckewelder spoke:

"I had word from a trustworthy runner today. Girty and his captives have not been seen in the Delaware towns."

"It is unlikely he would take them to the towns," remarked Edwards. "Why do you suppose he captured Jim?"

"For Pipe, perhaps. The old wolf is always snapping his teeth, and he is particularly opposed to Christianity— What's that?"

A low whistle had sounded from the bushes near the creek bank. The younger men got up to investigate but Heckewelder detained them.

"Wait," he said. "There's no telling what that may mean."

They waited with breathless interest. Presently the whistle was repeated. An instant later the tall figure of a man stepped from behind a thicket. The stranger waved a hand as if asking them to be cautious and come to him.

They went toward the thicket and when they had come within a few paces of the man Mr. Wells uttered an exclamation.

"It's the man who guided my party to the village —it's Wetzel!"

The others looked at the hunter with great curiosity. His buckskin garments were wet and torn and covered with burrs. Bloodstains showed on his hunting-shirt.

"Wetzel?" Heckewelder asked timidly.

The hunter nodded and stepped back behind the bush. Bending over, he lifted something from the ground.

It was a girl—Nell Wells. She was very white, but alive! A faint, glad smile lighted up her features.

Not a word was spoken. Mr. Wells took the girl in his arms with a tender expression.

"She's well and unharmed," said Wetzel, "but worn out. I've carried her fer ten miles or more."

"God bless you, Wetzel!" exclaimed the old missionary. "Nell—Nell, can you speak?"

"Yes, Uncle dear," came the faint answer. "I'm all right."

"Kate? What of her?" whispered George Young.

"I did my best," said Wetzel simply.

"Tell us," broke in Heckewelder.

"We trailed 'em, and got away with this lass," said the hunter. "The last I saw of Joe he was braced up ag'in' a rock, fightin' like a wildcat. I tried to cut Jim loose as I was goin' past, but I 'spect the wust fer the brothers—and the other lass."

"Can we do nothing?" asked Mr. Wells.

"Nothin'."

"Wetzel," inquired Heckewelder, "does the capturing of James Downs signify anything special to you?"

"Reckon it does. Pipe and his white and Injun friends are ag'in' Christianity and they're out to smash the mission."

"Do you think we are in danger?"

"Reckon so."

"What would you advise?"

"Pack up what you kin take, bring the lass, and come with me. I'll see you back to Fort Henry."

Heckewelder began to pace nervously back and forth. Young and Edwards gazed uneasily at one another. Mr. Wells uttered an angry exclamation.

"You ask us to fail in our duty? Never! Should we go back to the white settlements and admit we were afraid to continue teaching the Gospel to the Indians? You cannot understand Christianity if you advise us to do that! You have no religion—you are a killer of Indians."

"No, I ain't a Christian, and I am a killer of Injuns," Wetzel declared in his deep voice. "I don't know nothin' much 'cept the woods, and if thar's a God fer me He's out thar under the trees. You're the fust man as ever called me a coward, Mr. Wells, but I'll overlook it, 'count of yer callin'. I advised ye to go back to Fort Henry 'cause if ye don't go now the chances are ag'in' yer ever goin'."

"I thank you for your advice," answered Mr. Wells steadily, "and I bless you for the rescue of this girl.

But I cannot leave my work, and I cannot admit that all we have done is useless. We have converted Indians—saved their immortal souls. Have we not therefore done some good here?"

"It's 'cordin' to how ye look at it. The bark of an oak is different 'cordin' to the side we see it from. I 'low hatin' Injuns as I do is no reason why you oughtn't try to convert 'em. But you're bringin' on a war. The Injuns won't let this Village of Peace, with its fields and shops and workin' redskins, stay here. It's ag'in' their nature. You're only sacrificin' yer Christian Injuns."

"What do you mean?" asked Mr. Wells, startled.

"I mean enough—and I'm ready to guide you to Fort Henry."

"I'll never go," said Mr. Wells stubbornly.

Wetzel looked at the other men. It was clear that he knew some terrible danger threatened the Village of Peace.

"I believe you, Wetzel," said Heckewelder, his face white, "but I cannot go."

"I will stay," said Young steadfastly.

"And I," added Edwards.

Wetzel nodded and turned to leave. Young grasped him by the arm. The young missionary's face was drawn and haggard as he looked intently at the hunter.

"Listen, Wetzel," he began, his voice low and tense with feeling. "I am a teacher of God's word, and I am as sincere in my lifework as you are in yours. I may die here, and fill an unmarked grave, but I'll do the best I can. This is the life that destiny has marked out for me, and I do not regret it now. But at this moment I would give everything I have to be a man like you.

"You are the man to kill Girty! Rid the frontier of this monster! Kill him, Wetzel—kill him! Trail him without let-up, and when you find him have no mercy!"

Wetzel did not say a word. He stretched out his long arm and gripped the young missionary's shoulder. Then he stepped past a tree, and bounding lightly as a deer, he cleared the creek and disappeared in the bushes.

Mr. Wells carried Nell to his cabin, where she lay with pale face, quiet and unmoving. She managed to swallow the nourishing drink that an old Indian nurse forced between her lips. She even smiled weakly when the missionaries spoke to her. But she would not talk, and she seemed to sink into a state of listlessness in which nothing could interest her.

"Dave, I'm afraid we're going to lose Nell," said Young one evening several days after the girl's return. "Wetzel said she hadn't been harmed, but something is certainly wrong with her. It must be her mind—if we can't do something to brighten her up and make her forget, why—"

"We've done everything we can. If she could only

be brought out of this trance!"

"Well, I have an idea. Have you noticed that Mr. Wells has been failing lately?"

"Yes, I have—I'm afraid this border life is too much for him. He's no longer young."

"Well, Dave, I think we might stir Nell back into life by telling her that her uncle's health is bad and he needs her."

"It's worth a try."

A knock on the door interrupted their conversation.

"Come in," called Edwards.

The door opened, and in came Jim Downs.

"Jim!" they both exclaimed, rushing to him.

He wrung the hands of his two friends, but no answering smile lighted his thin face.

"You're not hurt?" asked Edwards.

"No, I'm uninjured."

"Tell us what happened. Did you see your brother? Did you know that Wetzel rescued Nell?"

"Wingenund set me free, in spite of the fact that many of his chiefs demanded my death. But he kept Joe a prisoner and intends to have him killed, because he was Wetzel's companion. I saw Wetzel come into the glade where Girty and the Indians had us tied, break through, and get away with Nell."

"What about Kate?" faltered Young, his face ashen.

"George, I wish I could tell you what has hap-

pened to her, but I can't. She was well when I saw
her last. She wasn't taken into the Indians' camp
with Joe and me, though. Girty left us before we got
there, and took her with him. I—I'm afraid he means
to make her his slave."

Young sank down and buried his face in his hands.

"Did you say Wetzel has come in with Nell?" Jim
asked, turning to Edwards.

"Yes, he brought her back," Edwards answered
slowly.

"I'd like to see her," said Jim, moving toward the
door.

"Don't go," Edwards begged. "Wait—we must see
what's best to be done. Wait till Heckewelder comes
—he'll be here soon. Nell thinks you're dead, and
the shock of seeing you might be bad for her."

At that moment Heckewelder came in, and shook
hands warmly with Jim.

"The Delaware runner told me you were here. I
am overjoyed that Wingenund set you free—it is a
good sign. But I'm sorry indeed about your brother.
Are you well?"

"Well—but miserable. I'd like to see Nell."

"It'll be exactly the tonic for her," exclaimed
Heckewelder. "She has been sad and dispirited and
we haven't been able to interest her in anything.
Come at once."

Heckewelder had taken Jim's arm and started for
the door when he caught sight of Young, still sitting

with bowed head. Turning to Jim, he whispered, "Kate?"

Jim nodded. "Girty didn't take her to the Indian camp. I don't know what's become of her."

Just then Young raised his face. "I—can't stand it!" he said hoarsely. Staggering into the next room, he threw himself down on his bed.

Heckewelder was a mild, pious man ordinarily, but now he showed strong emotion. His face became white and twisted with rage.

"It's bad enough to have these renegades plotting and working against religion—to have them sow discontent, spread lies, make the Indians think we are trying to fool them—all that is bad enough, but to doom an innocent white woman to a life of slavery! That is monstrous."

"Is there no hope of getting Kate back?" Jim asked.

"None. Girty is surrounded by his savages. He'll lie low for a while. I can't believe—"

"Wetzel has gone on Girty's trail," broke in Edwards. "I'm sure of that, from his manner when he left us."

"Wetzel may avenge her. That is the only hope," said Heckewelder. Then: "Hello!"

The exclamation was caused by the appearance of Young, who entered the room with a rifle in his hand.

"George, where do you think you're going with

that gun?" demanded Edwards, grasping his friend's arm.

"I'm going after her," answered Young wildly.

"Come, George, come," Heckewelder said soothingly. "You are frantic with grief now. So are the rest of us. But calm yourself. Why, man, you're a preacher, not a hunter. You'd get lost and starve in the woods before you got halfway to the Indian town. Don't make this terrible thing worse by throwing your life away. Bear up the best you can, for the sake of our work. We can, perhaps, check this savagery, but not by fighting. We must make sacrifices, for the sake of the future."

Gently he removed the rifle from Young's hands and led him back into the other room. Closing the door, he turned to the other two with a sad smile.

"Think of George starting out to kill Girty!" said Edwards wonderingly. "I doubt if he's ever fired a gun in his life."

"All of us would do the same, if we followed our hearts!" retorted Heckewelder, turning fiercely upon him. "Man, we have a village of Christians to look after! What will become of them? I'm afraid we've got all we can do here to outwit these border outlaws. Simon Girty is plotting our ruin—I heard it today from a friendly Delaware runner."

The missionary raised his head as if calling upon some power above.

"Curse the Girtys!" he cried out passionately.

He stood there for a minute, his face working as he got his feelings under control.

"Come," he said, his voice trembling. "We'll go to see Nell."

The three entered Mr. Wells's cabin. The old man, who was pacing to and fro with his hands clasped behind him, greeted Jim with glad surprise.

"We want Nell to see him," whispered Hecke-welder. "It should do her good."

They all followed him into the next room. A torch flickering over the mantel shelf lighted the room with a fitful flare.

Jim saw the girl lying on a bed. Her eyes were closed, the long dark lashes sharply defined against the marble paleness of her skin.

"Stand behind me," Heckewelder whispered to him. Then to the girl, softly: "Nellie."

Her eyes opened, but they showed neither interest nor recognition.

"Nellie, can you understand me?"

The eyes flickered, as if to signal that she did.

"Listen, girl—you have had a bad shock. But you are mistaken in what you have feared. Do you under-stand?—you have been wrong!"

Puzzled, questioning doubt showed in the eyes.

"See, I have brought Jim to you!"

Heckewelder stepped aside as Jim fell on his knees beside the bed. He took her hands in his.

The doubt in the girl's eyes changed to gladness.

"Jim?" she whispered.

"Yes, Nell—it's Jim, alive and well. Jim—come back to you!"

Color came back to her cheeks. One of her hands reached to touch his face.

"Jim," she murmured.

"Nell," said her uncle, stepping forward, "don't you know me?"

"Uncle!" she exclaimed suddenly, and sat straight up in bed. She gazed wildly at the others. "Was it all a bad dream?"

Mr. Wells looked helplessly at Heckewelder, who was intently studying the expression on Nell's face.

"Part of it was a dream," he said.

"Then—then that awful man did take us away?"

"Yes, Nell, but you're safe now—safe at home."

A choking cry escaped her, and then came relief in a flood of tears.

CHAPTER TWENTY

VISITORS TO THE VILLAGE

Early on the following day Heckewelder, astride his horse, appeared at the door of Edwards's cabin.

"How is George?" he inquired, when Edwards came to the door.

"He had a bad night, but he's sleeping now. I think he'll be all right after a while."

"Dave, I leave matters here in your charge. I'm off to Goshocking to join Zeisberger. Things there demand our immediate attention."

"How long do you expect to be gone?"

"A few days, possibly a week. If there's any unusual disturbance among the Indians, or if Pipe and his tribe show up, send a fast runner to warn me. But I'm very encouraged by Wingenund's attitude. His freeing Jim against the wishes of his chiefs is a sure sign of his friendliness. I rather suspect he has a secret interest in Christianity."

"I take a hopeful view myself," replied Edwards.

"We can only trust in Providence and do our best." Heckewelder turned his horse. "Good-by."

"Godspeed!" Edwards called after him, and returned to his task of getting breakfast.

He stayed indoors all that day, except for a few moments when he ran over to Mr. Wells's cabin to ask after Nell's condition. He was relieved to learn that she was so much better that she was moving about the house. To his further satisfaction, Young had rallied and, although very quiet, seemed to be pulling himself together.

Nell put aside her grief over Kate's unknown fate by devoting herself to her uncle. He had aged much in the past months and now it was up to her alone to see that he did not suffer.

Jim seemed somehow changed since his return from the Delaware camp. Although he went back to work with his old determination, he was not nearly as successful as he had been before. This worried him deeply. To Nell he tried to show his affection not by words of love but by little acts of kindness and attention to her needs and those of her uncle.

The days following Heckewelder's departure were ones of slight activity. The weather was fair, but the number of visiting Indians gradually lessened. Finally there came the day when not a single Indian from the outlying villages came to hear the preaching.

Jim continued to speak, as usual. After several days had passed with none but already converted Indians in the congregation he began to feel uneasy.

Finally Jim went to consult old Glickhican. He found the Delaware at work in the potato patch.

"Glickhican, can you tell me why no more Indians have come here lately?"

"Glickhican saw a blackbird flitting in the shadow of the moon. The bird hovered above the Village of Peace, but sang no song."

The old Delaware would give no other than this strange reply.

After a while Jim returned to his cabin, decidedly worried. He did not at all relish Glickhican's reply. It seemed to mean that a cloud was rising on the horizon of the Village of Peace. He told his fears to Young and Edwards and following a long discussion it was decided that they should send for Heckewelder.

A runner was dispatched to Goshocking. In due time the Indian returned with the startling news that Heckewelder had left that village days before, as had all the savages there except the few converted ones. The same was true of the adjoining town, Sandusky. There was no news at all of Zeisberger.

The missionaries were now thoroughly alarmed, but they concealed it from Nell and her uncle. That night the three of them went to bed with heavy hearts.

The next morning at daybreak Jim was awakened from a sound sleep by someone calling at his window. Hurriedly getting out of bed, he saw Edwards standing outside in the gray light.

"What's the matter?"

"Matter enough! Hurry and get into your clothes," replied Edwards. "As soon as you're dressed rouse Mr. Wells and Nell, but try not to frighten them."

"But what's the trouble?" Jim persisted as he began to dress.

"The Indians are pouring into the village as thick as falling leaves in autumn."

Edwards's statement proved to be almost literally true. As the rising sun dispelled the mist it shone on long lines of marching braves, mounted warriors, and hundreds of pack horses swarming in from the forests.

The missionaries watched from their windows with bated breath. They scanned the long lines of dusky forms with fear and wonder.

Once in the clearing, the savages began unpacking. Long rows of tepees sprang up—they had come to stay! The solid masses of incoming red men did not lessen until noon; then a few straggling bands marked the end of the invading host. And among them all there was not a child or a maiden or a squaw.

Jim guessed their number to be six or seven hundred, more than had ever before visited the village at one time. They were mostly Delawares, though there were many Shawnees and a few Hurons.

It was soon evident that the Indians did not intend any hostile moves, for the present at least. They

Hundreds of Indians Entered the Village

busied themselves about their tepees and campfires.

After talking it over with his fellow missionaries, Jim went ahead with the afternoon service. He spoke to the largest congregation that had ever gathered before him. The sermon was followed by a brooding silence which Jim feared boded no good.

Four white men dressed as Indians had listened attentively to his sermon. He recognized Simon Girty, Elliott, and Deering, and learned from Edwards that the fourth one was the notorious renegade McKee. After the service these men went through the village, stalking into shops and cabins as though they were on a tour of inspection.

Jim hurried back to the Wellses' cabin. Nell and her uncle showed their fright and Jim's assurance that there was no real cause for fear failed to relieve them.

He was sitting at the doorstep with Mr. Wells and Edwards when Girty and his comrades came toward them. The renegade leader was a tall man with a dark, strong face. He did not appear as brutal as his brother. His companions presented contrasts. Elliott was a small, spare man with a cunning expression. McKee's looks fitted his reputation. Deering was a fit mate for the absent Jim Girty.

"Where's Heckewelder?" Girty asked curtly.

"He started out for the Indian towns on the Muskingong," Edwards replied, "but we've had no word from either him or Zeisberger."

"When d'ye expect him?"

"I can't say—perhaps tomorrow, perhaps in a week."

"He's in charge here, ain't he?"

"Yes, but he left things in my hands while he's away. Is there anything I can do for you?"

"I reckon not." The renegade turned to his friends. They talked in low tones for a moment. Then McKee, Elliott, and Deering went toward the newly erected tepees.

"Girty, do you mean to do us any ill?" Edwards asked earnestly. He had met the man several times and did not hesitate to question him.

"I can't say as I do," the renegade replied. "But I'm ag'in' this redskin preachin' and have been all along. The Injuns are mad clear through, and I ain't blamin' 'em. This missionary work has got to be stopped, one way or another. Now I want to say this—I ain't quite forgot I was white once, and I believe you fellers are honest. I'm willin' to go outer my way to help you git away from here."

"But why should we go away? We hurt no one— we're only doing good. Why should we go?"

" 'Cause there's liable to be some trouble," Girty answered meaningly.

Edwards turned slowly to Mr. Wells and Jim. The old missionary was trembling. Jim was pale, but not from fear. His voice rang out:

"Thank you, Girty, but we'll stay."

CHAPTER TWENTY-ONE

HOSTILE CHIEFS

"Jim, come out here," called Edwards at the window of Mr. Wells's cabin.

Jim rose from the breakfast table and went outside, to find Edwards standing by the door with an Indian brave. He was a Wyandot, lightly built and wiry, and Jim quickly recognized him as a runner.

The Indian handed him a small packet and he unwound a few folds of some oily skin to find a square piece of birchbark, upon which were scrawled the following words:

Rev. J. Downs. Greeting.

*Your brother is alive and safe. Whispering Winds rescued him by taking him as her husband. Leave the Village of Peace. Pipe and Half King have been influenced by Girty.—*ZANE.

"Well, what do you think of that?" cried Jim, handing the message to Edwards. "Thank heaven Joe is safe!"

Edwards read the note. "Zane?" he pondered over the signature. "Must be the Zane who married Tarhe's daughter."

"Joe married to that Indian girl—" mused Jim. "Of all the wonderful things—but what will Nell think?"

"We're getting warnings enough, do you appreciate that?" Edwards demanded, pointing at the note.

"Edwards, I'm afraid these bordermen see what we will not admit. We ministers have such hope and trust in God that we cannot realize the dangers of life. Our work may have been in vain."

All this time the runner had stood near by, waiting. Presently Edwards asked him if he had something else to tell.

"Redman—go by—paleface." He held up both hands and closed his fists several times, to show how many men he had seen. "Here when sun high."

With that he loped away with an easy, swinging stride.

"What did he mean?" asked Jim.

"A party of white men are approaching and will be here by noon. Let's go in and tell the others."

The runner's report proved to be correct. Shortly before noon signals from Indian scouts warned of the approach of a party of white men. Girty's forces must have had prior knowledge of their coming, for the signals created no excitement. Soon several Delaware scouts appeared, guiding a large party of frontiersmen.

It was an expedition under Captain Williamson, which had been after a tribe of raiding Chippewas.

It included men who had served in the garrison at Fort Pitt, along with hunters and backwoodsmen from Yellow Creek and Fort Henry.

The captain was a rough, bluff borderman, hardened by long years of frontier life. He had surprised the raiders and nearly all of them had been killed. Returning eastward, he had passed through Goshocking, where he had heard that trouble threatened the Village of Peace.

The worried missionaries welcomed the newcomers heartily. Beds were made in several of the newly erected cabins. Everything possible was done for the comfort of the frontiersmen. Edwards conducted Captain Williamson through the shops and schools.

"Well!" he ejaculated. "I'm durned if I ever expected to see a redskin work!"

"We've been alarmed by the presence of Girty and his men," Edwards said. "He's warned us to leave, although there have been no actual threats. What do you think?"

"Hardly 'pears to me they'd bother you preachers," replied the captain thoughtfully. "They're ag'in' the Christian Injuns, that's plain."

"But why have we been warned to go?"

"Only nateral, seein' they're ag'in' the preachin'."

"Do you think the converted Indians are in danger?"

"Well, they might let 'em go back to the tribes, but I don't s'pose these good Injuns'd want to go.

Anyways, Girty'd be afraid they'd spread Christianity."

"I suppose you think we'd do well to leave here."

"I sartin do. We're hittin' out fer Fort Henry soon and you'd best come along with us."

"Captain, we intend to stick it out here."

"You can't do no good stayin' here. Pipe and Half King won't stand fer singin', prayin' redskins, 'specially when they've got all this cattle and grain."

"Wetzel said much the same."

"That so? I met him and Jack Zane back a few miles. They must be layin' fer somebody, 'cause when I asked 'em to come along with us they 'lowed they had work as had to be done. Anyways, if Wetzel told me to do a thing, by gum I'd do it!"

"As ordinary men, we might take such advice, but as preachers we feel that it is our duty to stay here and do all we can for these Christian Indians. One thing more, Captain—will you help us?"

"Reckon I'll stay here to see the thing out," Williamson answered.

Meanwhile, Jim had made the acquaintance of a young minister named John Christy, who had lost his sweetheart in one of the Chippewa raids and had come with the expedition in the hope of rescuing her.

"How long have you been out?" Jim asked.

"About four weeks. Martha was captured five weeks ago yesterday. I joined Williamson's band on the chance I'd find her. But not a trace, though we found a bunch of Indians over on the Walhonding and slaughtered nearly all of them."

Jim told the story of his own capture by Jim Girty, the rescue of Nell, and the missing Kate.

"Do you suppose Jim Girty could have got your girl?" he ended.

"It's hardly likely. There are a dozen or more renegades on the border, all about equally bad."

"Then it's a common occurrence—this kidnaping girls from the settlements?"

"Oh, yes, and not only girls—women and children as well. They're carried into captivity without much hope of ever returning. They are little better than slaves and are treated pretty harshly, though there are a few who seem to have got along fairly well, fitting themselves into the life of the Indians. But most of them die soon, and a rescue is made very seldom."

"If you have so little hope of finding your sweetheart, why are you with this band of hunters?"

"Revenge!"

Jim was astonished. "And you are a preacher?"

"I was a preacher," Christy replied, his face darkening. "Now I am thirsting for vengeance. Wait until you really learn what this frontier life means! You're new here still—you have lived in this quiet village, with everything serene. In two years on the border all this strife and cruelty have hardened me so that I yearn to spill the blood of the devil who took my sweetheart from me. Any pioneer who expects to survive out here has to be a fighter, ready to take his foe's life before that foe can take his!''

The calm and peaceful days of the village were no more. A French trader showed up with a supply of cheap firewater. The unwanted visitors became insulting and abusive. Loudly they denounced the Christian Indians and their new God. This new religion, they said, made strong men into weak women. Boldly they slaughtered cattle and stole from the corn cribs.

All this time Girty and Elliott consulted often with Pipe and Half King. The fate of the village seemed to rest with these two chiefs.

Finally Heckewelder returned to the village, to the great relief of the other missionaries. He was weary and travel-worn. Three times he had been held up and assaulted on the way to Goshocking. Shortly before he got there a roving band of Chippewas found him and forced him to stay in their camp for a day and a half. While he was there a renegade ran off with a white woman they had with them. The one good piece of news he brought back was that Zeisberger was safe in a Moravian town some miles west.

He was bewildered by the great array of hostile Indians in the Village of Peace. Chiefs who had once been friendly to him now drew back coldly. Washington was dead, they said; the American armies were cut to pieces; the few thousand who had escaped the British were gathering at Fort Pitt to steal the Indians' land.

Heckewelder strongly denied all this, knowing that it had been invented by Girty and Elliott. He wore out his skill and patience trying to show Pipe that it was wrong. Half King refused even to listen. The other chiefs maintained a cold silence. Wingenund had showed up, but took no part in the councils.

"I'm completely fagged out," Heckewelder finally confessed, dropping into a chair in Edwards's cabin.

"Lie down and get some rest," Edwards urged him. "You're tired out and discouraged. Perhaps things are not so hopeless. The presence of all these frontiersmen should encourage us."

"What can they do?" Heckewelder cried bitterly. "I tell you I've never seen the Indians so cold and hostile. They act like men who have already decided on their course, and are only waiting."

"For what?" asked Jim after a long silence.

"God only knows. It may be for—for a reason the thought of which makes me feel sick."

"Tell us," said Edwards quietly.

"My friends, I pray I am wrong. God help us if my fears are correct. I am afraid the Indians are waiting for Jim Girty."

CHAPTER TWENTY-TWO

Simon Girty lolled on a blanket in Half King's tepee. He was alone, waiting for his allies. Rings of white smoke curled lazily from his lips as he puffed on a long Indian pipe.

Simon Girty's face was bronzed and hard. It would have been called handsome except for the deep lines that had come there with years of revolt and bitterness. In spite of the cruelty there it was not a bad face. There were still some traces of a man in whom kindlier feelings had once ruled.

In a reckless moment Girty had deserted his military post at Fort Pitt and become an outlaw. Before that he had been an able soldier and a respected man. When he realized that he had taken a step from which there was no coming back and that his former friends condemned him, he plunged into a desperate war against his own race.

Both his brothers had long been border outlaws whose only safety from the outraged pioneers lay in the faraway camps of hostile tribes. They seemed to revel in being even more ferocious than the worst

Indians, and it was largely to their evil deeds that Simon Girty owed his own bad reputation.

Now a slight tremor of the ground caused him to turn his head. Half King, magnificent in his colorful trappings, entered the tepee. He squatted in a corner and smoked in silence.

Soon another chief stalked in and seated himself. It was Pipe. His face had none of the intelligence that shone from Wingenund's. The thin, tightly closed lips looked as if they could relax only to utter some savage command.

"White Chief is idle today," said Half King.

"I am waiting. Girty is slow but sure," answered the renegade.

"The eagle sails slowly round and round, up and up," remarked Half King, "until his eye sees all, until he knows his time. Then he folds his wings and swoops down from the blue sky like forked fire. So does White Chief. But Half King grows impatient."

"Today decides the fate of the Village of Peace," answered Girty, unruffled.

Half King and Pipe both uttered expressions of approval.

An hour passed. The renegade and the two Indians smoked in silence.

A horseman rode up to the tepee entrance, dismounted, and came in. It was Elliott. His buckskin suit showed the effects of hard riding through the thickets.

"Hullo, Bill," Girty greeted his lieutenant. "Any sign o' Jim?"

"Nary a sign. He ain't been seen near the Delaware camp. He's after that feller who married Whispering Winds."

"I was afeerd so. Jim's monkeyin' with a tenderfoot who'll be a bad man to handle if he has half a chance. He hadn't ought to let personal revenge interfere at a time like this!"

"Jim said he'd be here today, didn't he?"

"Today's as long as we 'lowed to wait."

"He'll come, all right. Where's Jake and Mac?"

"Out around somewhere, raisin' the devil."

Shortly after this McKee and Deering entered the tepee and squatted, Indian-fashion. Both had bloodshot eyes and appeared to be suffering from the effects of the French trader's firewater.

"Bad time fer drinkin'," Girty disapproved.

"What's it to ye?" Deering growled. "I'm here to do yer work and I'll do it, all right, don't ye fear."

"Well, don't get careless," Girty said warningly. "I don't want you to blab all you know. We've got lots o' work to do without gettin' into trouble with Williamson's bunch. Bill, tie up the tent flaps and we'll get to council."

Elliott rose to carry out the order and had pulled in the deerhide flaps when one of them was jerked outward to disclose Jim Girty.

Pipe and Half King grunted their pleasure, and

Simon Girty greeted him with a "Hullo."

" 'Pears I'm in time fer the picnic," Jim said with a ghastly, crooked grin.

Elliott closed the flaps, first having ordered an Indian guard to prevent anyone from coming near the tepee.

"Listen," said Simon Girty, speaking low in the Delaware tongue. "The time is ripe. We have come here to destroy forever the influence of the white man's religion. It has already been decided that we shall drive away the missionaries and burn the Village of Peace."

He paused and leaned forward before he continued: "One thing remains to be decided: what shall we do with the Christian Indians?"

Pipe raised his war club, struck it on the ground, and handed it to Half King. Half King took the club and repeated the action.

Simon Girty glanced at his brother questioningly.

"Feed 'em to the buzzards," croaked Jim.

Simon Girty frowned in thought. "No," he said finally; "let us drive away the missionaries, burn the village, and take the Indians back to camp. We'll keep them there—they'll soon forget what they've been taught."

"Pipe does not want them," declared that chief.

"Christian Indians shall never sit around Half King's fire," cried the Huron.

Simon Girty knew the crisis had come. However

cruel his life and great his misdeeds, he still possessed some shreds of honor. He wanted to burn the village and wreck the power of the mission but he would prefer to do it without shedding blood. Yet he could not check the growing strength of the Christians without the help of Pipe and Half King. To these savages a thing was either right or wrong. He had sown the seeds of unrest in their savage breasts, and the fruit was their call for death.

If he did not destroy the Village of Peace, the missionaries would soon get such a grasp on the tribes that their hold would never be broken. He could not allow that, for the growth of religion would mean his own downfall. The border must remain hostile to the whites, or it could no longer be his home.

He knew he must sacrifice the Christians or lose his own power. He knew the converted Indians were innocent, but that weighed little against his determination to preserve his own position. Still, he shrank from a deed that would attach even greater horror to his name.

Half King waited long for Girty to speak. When he remained silent the wily Huron suggested they take a vote on the question.

"Let us burn the Village of Peace, drive away the missionaries, and take the Christians back to the Delaware towns—all without spilling blood," repeated Girty stubbornly.

"I say the same," declared Elliott, refusing the war

club which Half King held out to him.

"Me, too," voted McKee as Girty shot him a light-ninglike glance of warning.

Deering, however, grasped the war club and pounded it gleefully on the ground. "Kill 'em all, kill everybody!" he laughed coarsely.

Pipe repeated his former performance, as did also Half King. The club was then passed to Jim Girty.

Three had voted to save the Christians, and three for death. Six pairs of burning eyes were fixed on Jim Girty. Simon Girty silently cursed the fates. He dared not try to influence his brother's vote in the presence of the two chiefs.

Jim Girty was in no hurry. He was glorying in his power. Slowly he took up the war club, studying it as if it were something he had never seen before. The silence of the grave reigned in the tepee.

Then suddenly he raised the club on high and crashed it violently to the ground.

"Feed the Christians to the buzzards!"

CHAPTER TWENTY-THREE

THE DEATH DECREE

When the first ruddy rays of the rising sun crimsoned the eastern sky, Wetzel slowly made his way down a rugged hill far west of Beautiful Spring. He stopped in a little cave under a projecting stone and, laying aside his rifle, began to gather twigs and sticks. When he finally kindled a flame it blazed hotly without making smoke.

He sharpened a green stick, took some strips of meat from his pocket, and roasted them over the hot flame. Then, having eaten, he put out the fire, and found a spot on top of the ledge where he commanded a good view of the surroundings. Settling himself, he soon was sleeping lightly.

About noon he awoke, stretched, and took a position on the front of the ledge where he could easily see below. He listened to the sounds of the forest—the soft breeze that fluttered the leaves, the rain-call of the tree frogs, the caw of crows from distant hilltops.

Suddenly he raised his head. A whistled note had come from far down the shaded hollow. He whistled a note in answer, as deep and clear as the one which had caught his attention.

In a few minutes the figure of a tall man appeared among the laurels down the slope. He climbed the ridge and the rocky ledge and faced Wetzel. It was Jonathan Zane.

"Jack, I expected you afore this," Wetzel said.

"Couldn't make it sooner," replied Zane. "After we left Williamson and separated, I had to swing around a band of several hundred redskins makin' for the Village of Peace. I went back ag'in but couldn't find any sign of the trail we're huntin'. Then I made for the meetin' place here. I been goin' for ten hours, and I'm hungry!"

"Got some b'ar ready cooked," said Wetzel, handing him several strips of meat.

"What luck did you have?"

"Wal, I found Girty's trail—an old one—over here some eighteen or twenty miles, and follered it till it almost led me into the Delaware town. Finally came to a hut in a deep ravine. Thar I found the dead body o' Silvertip, the Shawnee I've been lookin' fer. Couldn't figger who done fer him, 'less him and Girty had a fallin' out.

"I hung around and seen Girty come back to the hut. He had ten Injuns with him and after a while they all made fer the west. I trailed 'em, but didn't calkilate it'd be wise to tackle the bunch single-handed, so I laid back.

"A mile or so from the hut, I come across hoss tracks mingled with the moccasin prints. 'Bout fifteen mile or so from the Delaware town Girty left his redskins and they went west, while he stuck to the hoss tracks. I was onto his game in a minute and cut across country fer Beautiful Spring. Got there ahead of him, too, and found Joe and Whisperin' Winds and the missionary's other niece. Joe was laid up with a bad knife wound, but was 'bout ready to travel ag'in. The white gal seemed kind o' dazed.

"I tried to ambush Girty, but the cuss winded me somehow, and all I got was a long shot at him as he turned tail. Follered him a ways, but he took to a crick and I didn't want to take the time to try and untangle his trail. Figgered Joe and the others needed help more. Went back to them and give 'em close directions fer gittin' back to Fort Henry by a little-used way, soon's Joe kin travel safe. I reckon Girty'll stay shy of 'em long's he thinks I'm still around these parts."

"Chances are he's gone back t' jine the renegade cutthroats and a horde of riled Injuns over at the Village of Peace."

"Reckon you're right."

A long silence followed. Jonathan finished his meal, drank from the spring, and wiped his mouth with the back of his hand.

"Lew, we're pretty good friends, ain't we?" he asked then.

"Jack, you and the colonel are all the friends I ever had, 'ceptin' Joe."

"I want to speak plain about this Jim Girty."

"Go ahead," said Wetzel, as the other hesitated.

"One day, not so long ago it was, we found an old friend of ours, murdered in cold blood. We trailed the coward that did it and found it was Jim Girty. I knew you'd been huntin' him for years and so I says, 'Lew, you or me?' and you says, 'Me.'

"Now the months have gone by, and Jim Girty's still at large. Today he's over there after them poor preachers. Lew, I say let me in on it with you. He always has a gang o' redskins with him—else you'd got him long ago. Two of us'll have a better chance to get him. Let me go with you—when it comes to a finish I'll stand aside while you give it to him. After he leaves the Village of Peace, we'll hit his trail, camp on it, and stick to it till it ends in his grave. What do you say?"

Zane's earnest voice ceased. Both men rose and stood facing each other. Then their big hands met in a grip of iron.

Turning their faces toward the west, the two hunters passed silently down the ridge into the depths of the forest. Darkness found them within rifle shot of the Village of Peace. Carefully they crawled to a position which would, in daylight, command a view of the clearing. While one stood guard, the other slept.

When dawn came they shifted their position to the top of a low, fern-covered cliff, from which they could see every movement in the village. All morning they watched.

The visiting savages were quiet. The missionaries moved about, in and out of the shops and cabins. The Christian Indians worked away in the fields. The renegade whites lolled in front of a big tepee.

"Things seem so quiet it makes me uneasy," Jonathan whispered to Wetzel.

After an hour of fruitless watching the deep pealing of the church bell broke the silence. The Christian Indians began to gather in the maple grove where services were always held in pleasant weather. This movement brought them within several hundred yards of the cliff where Jonathan and Wetzel lay concealed.

"There's Heckewelder walking with old man Wells," Jonathan whispered. "And there's Young and Edwards—and yes, there's that young missionary, Joe's brother. 'Pears to me they're foolish to hold services in the face of all them riled Injuns."

"Wuss'n foolish," Wetzel grunted.

"Look! There comes the whole crowd of hostile redskins—they've got their guns and they're painted up! Looks bad, Lew—not much friendliness about that bunch."

"They ain't intendin' to be peaceable."

"By gum, you're right—ain't one of 'em settin'

down. Some of 'em look mighty familiar—yes, there's Pipe, sure enough—and Kotoxen—and if there ain't Shingiss! He was reckoned friendly once."

"None of 'em's friendly," protested Wetzel.

"Look, Lew! Right behind Pipe—that's your old friend Wingenund. 'Pears to me we've rounded up all our old acquaintances."

The two bordermen saw the converted Indians seat themselves before the platform. The crowd of hostile Indians surrounded the glade on all sides except one, which was next to the woods.

"Look thar," whispered Wetzel, pointing off to the right of the maple glade.

Jonathan gazed in that direction and saw two savages stealthily slipping through bushes and behind trees. Presently they stopped on a little knoll perhaps a hundred yards from the glade.

"Them red devils are up to somethin' bad, sure enough," Jonathan groaned.

Satisfied that the two concealed savages were bent on some kind of mischief, the hunters once more turned their gaze to the maple grove.

"Ah—there's Simon Girty, the traitor! See him comin', Lew, with his precious gang. He's got the whole thing fixed, you can see that plain. There's Bill Elliott, and McKee—and who's that renegade with Jim Girty? Must be the feller we heard was with the Chippewas."

"Somethin' comin' off," Wetzel whispered, and

Two Savages Crept Through the Bushes

Jonathan felt him tremble.

"The missionaries are consultin'— Here comes
one, Edwards, I guess. Now there's an Injun stalkin'
over from the hostile bunch, some big chief or other
—it's Half King!"

The watchers saw the chief wave his arm and
speak with seeming harsh command to Edwards.
However, the missionary advanced to the platform
and raised his hand to address the Christians.

Crack!

A shot rang out from the thicket. Clutching at his
side, the missionary reeled back and fell.

"One of the skulkin' redskins has killed Edwards!"
Jonathan burst out. "No—he's not dead! He's get-
tin' up—mebbe he ain't hurt bad. Why, there's
Young comin' forward—of all the fools!"

Young had indeed faced the Indians. Half King
spoke to him as he had to the other missionary, but
Young raised his hand and began to speak.

Crack!

Another shot rang out, and Young threw up his
hands and fell heavily. The other missionaries
rushed toward him. Mr. Wells ran around the group,
wringing his hands.

"He was hard hit," Jonathan muttered tensely.
"You can tell that by the way he fell."

Lying silent and motionless, Wetzel did not reply.

"By all that's holy, here comes the other young
feller—Joe's brother! He'll get plugged too," Jona-

than went on, more to himself than to his friend. "I hoped he'd show some sense— Well, Heckewelder's pullin' him back—there's some good judgment, at last!"

Half King stepped before the Christian Indians and addressed them. In his hand was a black war club, which he shook as he talked.

Jonathan heard a slight click, and turned to see that Wetzel had cocked his rifle.

"Listen, Lew—mebbe it ain't good sense. We're after Girty, you remember, and it's a long shot from here—full three hundred yards. Let's wait and see what comes off."

"Jack, I can't help it. It'll make our job harder, but I can't help it. I kin put a bullet atween the Huron's eyes, an' I'm a-goin' to do it."

"But you can't do it, Lew—it's too far for any gun. Wait." Jonathan laid a hand on Wetzel's shoulder.

"Wait? Man, can't you see what the cuss is doin'?"

"What?" breathed Jonathan, turning his eyes back to the glade.

The converted Indians sat with bowed heads. Half King raised his war club and threw it to the ground in front of them.

"He's givin' the death decree!" hissed Wetzel.

Jonathan looked at Wetzel's face. Then he rose to his knees, as had Wetzel, and tightened his belt. He knew that in another instant they would be speeding away through the forest.

"Lew, my rifle's no good for that distance. Mebbe yours is—you ought to know. But go ahead—plug the cowardly redskin!"

Wetzel knelt on one knee and thrust the black rifle forward through the fern leaves. Slowly the fatal barrel rose to a level.

Jonathan fixed his keen gaze on the haughty face of Half King as he stood with folded arms in front of the Christians he had just condemned to death.

CHAPTER TWENTY-FOUR

THE BULLET FROM THE CLIFF

"Please don't preach today." Nell raised her eyes imploringly to Jim's face.

"Nell, I must conduct the services as usual. I cannot shirk my duty—cannot let these renegades see that I fear to face them."

"But I have such a queer feeling—I'm afraid. I can't bear to be left alone. Please don't leave me, Jim."

"Nell, what is it you fear?" Jim asked gravely, taking her hands.

"Oh, I don't know—everything. Uncle is getting weaker every day—look at Mr. Young: only a shadow of his former self—and all this anxiety is wearing Mr. Heckewelder out. And those Indians waiting—for we don't know what! And worst of all, I saw that awful renegade—the one who made away with poor Kate!"

She burst into tears and, sobbing, leaned on Jim's shoulder.

Jim's voice trembled as he said, "Nell, I've kept my courage only because of you."

She looked up quickly. Something in his pale face told her that now was the time to forget herself.

"Oh, I've been silly and selfish!" she cried. Turn-ing away, she wiped the tears from her eyes. "Go ahead, Jim—do your duty. I'll stand by and help all I can."

The missionaries were holding a meeting in Heckewelder's cabin. Zeisberger had returned that morning, and his cheerful, fighting spirit was what they had needed.

"Hold the service? I should say we will!" He waved his hands. "What have we to be afraid of?"

Heckewelder shook his head. "I don't know— All this silence, this ominous waiting, bewilders me—"

"Gentlemen," spoke up Jim, "our duty is plain. The faith these Christian Indians have in us is so absolute they have no fear. If we do not hold the service they will conclude we are afraid of Girty, and that would destroy our influence over them."

"I'm in favor of postponing the preaching for a few days," said Heckewelder. "I tell you I'm afraid of Girty's Indians—not for myself, but for these Christians that we love so well."

"You are our leader," responded Edwards. "We shall obey you. Still, I think we owe it to our converts to stick to our work until we are forced by violence to stop."

"Yes, but what form will that violence take?" cried Heckewelder. "You can't tell what these sav-ages mean to do!"

"Heckewelder, don't forget we went through all this once before," Zeisberger put in earnestly. "In '78 Girty came down on us like a wolf on the fold. He tried to frighten us with his painted fiends, and he failed. We stuck it out and won. Now he's trying the same game. Let us trust in God, stand against him, and hold our services as usual."

"Never give up," said Jim firmly.

"Gentlemen, you are right," said Heckewelder with a sigh. "You put me to shame. Whatever happens, we'll stick to our post. I am grateful to you for reviving the spirit in me. We'll hold the service to-day, and each one of us shall address the congregation in turn."

The deep, mellow peals of the church bell awoke the echoes. Scarcely had the sound died away in the forest when a line of Indians issued from the church and marched toward the maple grove—men, women, and children.

Glickhican, the old Delaware chief, headed the line. His step was firm, his head was erect, his face was calm. The faces of his followers also showed the steadfastness of their belief.

No sooner had the Christians reached the maple grove when from all over the clearing appeared hostile Indians, who took positions near the knoll where the missionaries always stood.

Heckewelder's faithful little band approached the

platform. As usual, the converted Indians seated themselves at the foot of the knoll. The other savages, all carrying weapons, crowded in close on each side.

Heckewelder hurried up just ahead of Simon Girty and his band of renegades. With them were Pipe and Half King, both of whom came slowly across the clearing, passed through an opening in the crowd, and stopped close to the platform.

Heckewelder came breathlessly up to his missionaries.

"Do not preach today—I have been warned again," he said in a low voice.

"Do you forbid it?" Edwards inquired.

"No, no—I can't do that—but I beg it of you. Wait —wait until the Indians are in a better mood!"

Without a word, Edwards left the group, stepped upon the platform, and turned to face the Indians.

At the same moment Half King stalked majestically from before his party, carrying a black, knotted war club. His evil gaze ran slowly over the Christians and then came to rest upon Edwards.

"Half King's orders are to be obeyed," he cried in the Indian tongue. "Let the paleface keep his mouth closed."

But Edwards, without a moment's hesitation, calmly lifted his hand and began speaking:

"Beloved Christians, we meet today as we have met before, as we hope to meet—"

Spang!

The whistling of a bullet over the heads of the Christians accompanied the loud report of a rifle. Edwards clutched his side, reeled back, and fell, breathing heavily.

For a moment no one moved or spoke. The missionaries were stricken silent with horror, the converts seemed turned to stone, and the hostile savages watched and waited.

"I feared this!" Heckewelder cried, running forward.

The others followed him. Edwards lay on his back, with a hand pressed to his side.

"Dave, Dave, are you badly hurt?" asked Heckewelder in a voice low with fear.

"No, it's—too far out to be—bad," panted Edwards, struggling to his feet with their aid. "Get me —water."

They helped him from the platform and laid him on the grass under a tree.

Pressing Edwards's hand, Young murmured something that sounded like a prayer, and then walked straight to the platform.

"Back, paleface!" roared Half King, waving his war club.

"Be silent, you Indian dog!" Young's voice rolled out on the quiet air, so powerful in its scorn that the hostile savages were awed, as the Christians were thrilled.

"Beloved Christians," Young began, "we have taught you how to live. If it is God's will, we can show you how to die—"

Spang!

Again came the whistling sound, with the bellow of a rifle. Young fell backward from the platform.

White-faced and shaking, the missionaries laid him beside Edwards and then stood in shuddering silence. A smile shone on Young's pale face. His lips moved.

"God's will," he whispered.

Jim looked down at him, then with face bloodless but resolute he marched toward the platform. Hecke-welder ran after him and dragged him back.

"No! No!" he cried. "Would you be killed?—Oh, I tried to prevent this!"

A long, fierce, victorious yell from hate-filled breasts pealed through the grove. All eyes turned to Half King. He paced to and fro before the Christian Indians.

"Blinded fools!" he cried. "The Huron is wise; he tells no lies. Many moons ago Half King urged you to leave this village, to forget the paleface God, to take your horses and flocks and return to your homes. You scorned my counsel. Now the sun has set for the Village of Peace. Pipe and the Huron are powerful. They do not fear the paleface God. They will burn the Village of Peace! Death to the Christians!"

With a passionate gesture Half King threw the black war club on the grass before the converts.

They heard the decree of death without flinching. Even the children were quiet.

"Oh, good heaven, it is worse than I thought!" moaned Heckewelder. "Murder—black murder—"

Following his outburst there was silence for a moment. Then a tiny cloud of blue-white smoke appeared above the ferns overhanging a cliff.

Crack!

Half King stood still for an instant as if he had been an image of stone. His haughty head then lost its erect poise. The fierceness faded from his dark face. He swayed and fell.

No one moved. It was as if no one breathed. The savages seemed to be awaiting another rifle shot—another visitation from the paleface's God.

But Jim Girty had recognized the ring of that rifle. In his craven fear he yelled:

"Le Vent de la Mort!"

The dreaded name aroused the savages from their trance into a fierce show of hatred. A tremendous yell rent the air. They reached for their weapons.

CHAPTER TWENTY-FIVE

THE LAST SERVICE

In the confusion the missionaries carried Young and Edwards into Mr. Wells's cabin. Heckewelder left them there and hurried away to talk to Captain Williamson. While Zeisberger attended to the wounded men, Jim barred the heavy door and shut the rude, swinging windows, to make the cabin a temporary refuge from prowling savages.

The clamor increased outside. Shrill yells and long, rolling war cries sounded above the din. The rhythmic stamp of moccasined feet and the thud of hatchets struck hard into trees indicated that the savages were working themselves up to a dangerous pitch.

In the front room of the cabin Edwards lay on a bed, his side exposed. Zeisberger was probing for the bullet.

"There, I have it," he said finally. "Hold still, Dave— There! Jim, wash and dress this wound. It isn't bad—he'll be all right in a couple of days. Now I'll take a look at George."

He hurried into the other room. Young lay quiet, eyes closed, breathing faintly. Zeisberger opened the shirt to expose the wound.

"How is he?" asked Jim, when Zeisberger came back and proceeded to wash his hands.

The other shook his head. "Shot through the right lung. I dressed the wound, but human skill cannot aid him now. He is in God's hands."

"That shot that brought down Half King—it seemed like a judgment of God," murmured Jim.

"It does seem so," said Zeisberger dryly, "but it came in the form of leaden death from Wetzel's unerring rifle. Do you hear all that yelling? Half King's death has set the Indians wild."

There came a gentle knock at the door, then the word, "Open," in Heckewelder's voice.

Jim unbarred the door. Heckewelder came in, with what seemed to be a sack of meal over his shoulder. He put the bag down, opened it, and lifted out a little Indian boy, who ran to Nell.

"Save Benny! Save Benny!" he cried as she clasped him tight in her arms.

Heckewelder's face was pale as he asked how Edwards was.

"I'm not badly off," answered Edwards himself, with a little smile.

"How about George?" whispered Heckewelder.

No one answered. They all followed Heckewelder into the other room, where Young lay in the same position as when first brought in.

"And to think I brought him here!" Heckewelder

exclaimed. "I persuaded him to come! Heaven forgive me!"

Zeisberger led him back to the larger room, the others following. Jim closed the door.

"Well, what's to be done?" said Zeisberger. "Tell us what you learned from Williamson."

Heckewelder sat down and covered his face with his hands. Finally he looked up, his expression one of despair.

"Gentlemen, the Village of Peace is doomed. I begged Captain Williamson to help us, but he refused. He said he dared not interfere. Then I implored him to at least say a word to Girty, but he would not even promise to do that. Girty has made his decision, and he has too many savages behind him to oppose."

"Where are the converts?"

"Imprisoned in the church—all except Benny here, whom I managed to hide in the sack. They asked for one hour in which to pray. It was granted. After that they will all—be massacred."

"Oh!" cried Nell. "How can they be so inhuman?" She lifted Benny up in her arms. "But they won't get you!" The child clung to her.

"They are scouring the clearing now for Christians, and they will search all the cabins."

"Will they come here?" asked Nell.

"Without a doubt. We must try to hide Benny. Let me think—where would be a good place? A dark corner of the loft, perhaps—"

"No, no," cried Nell, "they'll surely look there."

"Put him in a bucket and let him down in the well," suggested Edwards.

"No, no," she repeated.

"But we must decide, and in a hurry!"

"I'll save Benny," she said positively.

A heavy thump sounded on the door.

"Who's there?" called Heckewelder.

The thumping was repeated, this time with a hoarse command to open up.

"Quick! Hide Benny—it's as much as our lives are worth to have him found here!" Heckewelder whispered in desperation as he went to the door.

"All right, all right, in a moment," he called out, fumbling with the heavy bar.

A moment later he opened the door. As Jim Girty and Deering came in he turned to the others, his face haggard and uncertain.

Edwards lay on the bed, staring at the intruders with wide eyes. Mr. Wells sat with bowed head. Zeisberger was calmly whittling a stick. Jim sat bolt-upright, a hard light in his eyes. Nell leaned back against a table, eyes blazing from a face that was ghostly white.

Benny was not in sight.

Heckewelder turned slowly back to the men who had come in. He thought he had never seen such brutal faces.

"Wal, I reckon a preacher ain't a-goin' to lie," said Girty, carelessly waggling a tomahawk that he carried in one hand. "Have ye seen any Christian Indians round here?"

"Girty, we have hidden no Indians here," answered Heckewelder calmly.

"Wal, we'll have a look, anyway," said the renegade.

Slowly he surveyed the room with wolfish eyes. Then he and Deering proceeded to examine the room, looking into every box, behind the stove oven, and in the cupboard. They pulled the covers from the bed and kicked over a pile of stovewood. Then they passed into the next room, where, judging by the sounds, they made a thorough search.

At length they returned to the large room. At Girty's direction, Deering climbed the ladder to the loft and rummaged around up there for a few minutes.

"Wal, I reckon ye wasn't lyin' about it," Girty said with a leer when Deering came back down.

He and Deering started to go out. As they passed the girl, Deering motioned with his head toward her. Girty turned and fixed his evil glance on her.

Nell looked back at him, scorn and defiance in her gaze. After a moment's hesitation, he turned away without a word and the two renegades went out the door. Heckewelder closed it and dropped the bar in place.

Trembling violently, the girl uttered a low gasp of relief. Then with one hand she lifted up her skirt, and Benny walked out from under it. Thereupon she fell to the floor in a faint.

Mr. Wells and Jim worked over her anxiously. In a few moments she revived.

"Are you all right now?" Jim asked her.

"Yes," she whispered.

"I'm going out—first to see Williamson, then the Christians," he said, pale but calm.

"Don't go," Heckewelder begged. "I've tried everything—all of no use."

"I will go," Jim said firmly.

"Yes, Jim—go," said Nell in a low voice, looking up into his eyes.

He unbarred the door and went out.

"Wait—I'll go along with you," Zeisberger cried, starting after him.

As the two men emerged from the cabin they saw a fearful sight. The clearing was swarming with Indians, each one of whom seemed to be a painted, maddened demon. The day before they had been silent, standing or sitting quietly—if they moved at all it had been slowly and with dignity. Now, however, they yelled shrilly, running and leaping and brandishing their knives and tomahawks wildly. The blood lust was upon them.

"Awful!" exclaimed Zeisberger with a shudder. "Did you ever see human beings in such a state?"

"No," Jim replied, his face white.

"I saw a frenzy like this once before, but only in a small band of Indians, not a huge number like this. Several times I've seen savages preparing for the war path, against other tribes. They acted fierce, but they were nowhere near as bad as this. Think of it—every one of these painted devils honestly thinks it is his duty to murder those Christians. Girty has led up to this very cunningly, and now the time has come to let them loose."

"It means death for all?"

"I have given up any thought of escaping," Zeisberger said calmly. "I shall try to get into the church."

"I'll join you there as soon as I have seen Williamson," Jim responded.

He walked rapidly across the clearing to the cabin where Captain Williamson had headquarters. The frontiersmen stood about in groups, watching the savages with interest but seemingly with no concern.

"I want to see Captain Williamson," said Jim to a man who stood on guard by the door.

"He's inside," the man drawled.

Jim thought the voice was familiar and when he looked at him more closely he recognized Jeff Lynn, who had brought Mr. Wells's party to Fort Henry.

"Why, Lynn!" Jim exclaimed. "I'm glad to see you."

Jeff shoved out his big hand. "Wal, if 'tain't the

preachin' feller! Say, how's yer brother Joe?"

"I don't know," Jim confessed. "He ran off to the woods with Wetzel, was captured by Indians, and the last I heard of him he had married Wingenund's daughter."

"I'll be doggoned!" Jeff shook his grizzled head.

"I'm in a hurry," Jim went on. "Do you think Captain Williamson will stand still and let this sort of thing go on?"

"I'm afeered so, son."

The captain must have overheard them talking, for now he appeared at the cabin door, smoking a long pipe.

"Captain Williamson, I've come to beg you to save the Christians from this awful massacre that is threatened."

"Can't do nothin'," the captain grunted.

"Why, you have eighty men here!" Jim retorted.

"If we tried to interfere, Pipe would eat us alive in three minutes. You preacher fellers just don't understand this thing. You've got Girty as well as Pipe to deal with—and if you don't know them you're li'ble to be better acquainted by sundown."

"I don't care who they are! They're ruffians and savages, that's all! Won't you help us? We're men of your own race and we come to you for help—how can you refuse to give it?"

Jim was in a state of high excitement, his eyes flashing with indignation, but Captain Williamson could not be moved. Calmly he announced:

"I won't have nothin' to do with this business. The chiefs have condemned the village, and ain't nobody can stop 'em. If you fellers had only been careful, wouldn't no white blood have been spilled. I advise you all to lay low till it's over."

"Then will you let me speak to your men and try to get them to follow me?" Jim challenged.

"Heckewelder asked me that very same thing," Williamson admitted. "He made such a nuisance of himself about it that I finally put it up to the men. Eighteen of 'em said they'd follow him, and the rest didn't want to interfere."

"Eighteen!" Jim cried, aghast. "You're white men, and yet you'll stand by and see these innocent people murdered! Where's your humanity—your manhood? These converted Indians aren't savages any longer—they're Christians!"

Williamson made no reply. The men who had crowded around were also silent. Some of them looked at Jim, others watched the Indians who circled madly among the trees, shaking their weapons and howling. If any of them felt pity for the Christians, they did not show it. They had been hardened to such cruel scenes by years on the frontier.

As he turned from face to face to find everywhere the same cool indifference, Jim understood at last. These men were like Wetzel and Jonathan Zane— they believed that the only good Indian was a dead

Indian. Years of bloodshed and cruelty at the hands of the red men had made them incapable of feeling pity for any Indian, no matter what the situation.

His lips quivered as he said harshly, "I see. You don't believe a savage can be a Christian. You don't care if they are all murdered. Captain Williamson, you claim to be a soldier and a leader, but I say you are a coward! You—you are worse than Girty, for you could, if you wanted to, lead your men to stop this awful thing that is about to happen."

Williamson turned pale under this tongue-lashing, but he would not reply. The other bordermen likewise kept silent, staring at this raving preacher who did not know enough about the border to see things the way they saw them.

Baffled, Jim turned and walked away. As he did so, Jeff Lynn took his arm and when they were some distance from the others he said:

"Young feller, you sure give him what-fer. And mebbe you're right, from your side of the fence. But you ain't gone through what we have—we've lost many friends and relatives, and heard of so many murders by the redskins that we look on all of 'em as wild varmints to be killed on sight.

"I was watchin' ye when Edwards and the other feller got shot, and I seen ye had grit cl'ar through. I like that in a man. So when Heckewelder come over it was me as talked to the other fellers 'bout pitchin' in and helpin' you folks. Wal, all I could git interested was eighteen—and they wanted to fight simply fer the sake of fightin'. Now, Jeff Lynn is your friend, and I'm tellin' ye to just lay low till this is over."

Touched, Jim thanked the old borderman and left him. He hardly knew which way to turn. Finally he decided to make one more effort. He crossed the clearing to the renegades' tepee.

McKee and Elliott were sitting on a log. Simon Girty stood beside them, watching the scene before him. He had a strange, wild look in his eye, as if he had suddenly been aroused to fury. But Jim went straight toward him.

"Girty," he began, "I come to—"

"Git out, you meddlin' preacher!" Girty screamed, shaking his fist in Jim's face.

Jim turned away in dismay. He realized suddenly that his life, like those of the Christian Indians, meant no more to these renegades than a pinch of powder.

As he went toward the church he saw hundreds of savages bounding over the grass, shaking their weapons and whooping. They were beginning to gather around Girty's tepee.

He saw the fierce fire in their dark eyes as they streamed past him, saw the clenched teeth and the drawn-back lips. One of them flashed a knife before his face and another whirled a tomahawk close to his head, uttering a horrible yell.

"Git Out, You Meddlin' Preacher!"

He hurried on to the church. There was not an Indian anywhere near the log structure. Even the savage guards had gone. He entered the open door.

The Christian Indians were singing.

As full of misery and sickening dread as he was, Jim could not help responding to this wonderful scene. Never had these Indians sung the hymns so feelingly.

When the singing ended Zeisberger opened his Bible and read a verse, then said a short prayer. When it was over, the Indians rose and surrounded him. The men shook his hand, the women kissed his sleeve, and the children clung to his legs. Tears slid down Jim's cheeks as he witnessed their deep affection for this man of God.

Suddenly old Glickhican stepped up on the platform, raised his hand, and shouted an Indian word.

The men all stood proudly erect. The women slowly bowed their heads. Some of the children wailed. Then Glickhican pulled the bell rope. A deep mellow tone pealed out.

Glickhican had given the signal to the renegade and his followers that the Christians were ready.

For a moment no one moved. Then Jim burst out: "Come, man! We can't stay here."

He pulled Zeisberger away.

As they left the church and hurried toward the cabins they saw the crowd of savages in a black mass around Girty's tepee. The yelling and leaping were more violent than ever.

Heckewelder opened the door for them.

"Jim!" cried Nell. "Oh, I'm glad you're safe! See, this Indian has come to help us—"

Wingenund stood calmly inside the cabin near the door.

"What do you want, chief?" Zeisberger asked.

"Wingenund will show you the way to the big river," he answered in his deep voice.

"Run away?" cried Jim. "That would be cowardly! Heckewelder, you wouldn't go? Nor you?" He turned to Zeisberger. "Perhaps we can still save some of the Christians!"

"Save the yellow-hair," Wingenund said sternly.

"Jim," put in Nell, "the chief came to warn me of Girty. He plans to take me away as he did Kate. Oh, Jim, I can't stay here and face that! Please take me away!"

Jim took her hands. "I will," he said simply.

"Hurry!" said Heckewelder. "Here's a blanket full of things I packed for you." He went to the door and looked out.

"There they go—the pack of wolves! Jim Girty's running along in the lead—they're heading for the church."

He turned back, his hand before his eyes. "It's— the end."

"Where's Benny?" Jim demanded, lacing the hunting-coat he had flung about him.

"He's safely hidden. We'll get him away from here," Heckewelder replied. "Now's your time—go, and God speed you!"

"I'm ready," said Mr. Wells.

"There goes Wingenund," Heckewelder announced. "Follow him, and quickly! Good-by, good-by!"

Jim hurried Nell toward the bushes, where Wingenund's tall form could be seen going away. Mr. Wells followed them.

CHAPTER TWENTY-SIX

WETZEL'S VENGEANCE

At last, under the gold and red cover of the woods, the fugitives felt able to draw free breath. Still, they neither spoke nor looked back. Their guide hurried eastward with long strides, and they were almost forced to run to keep him in sight.

Wingenund had waited at the edge of the clearing for them and, taking the heavy pack from Jim, he had swung it easily over his shoulder and then proceeded to set a pace that was extremely hard to hold to. The young missionary half led, half carried Nell over the rough places. Mr. Wells labored along in the rear.

The Indian took a straight course through the woods. He made no effort to conceal their trail. Seemingly he thought the most important thing was to put as many miles as possible between them and the Village of Peace.

Gradually the ground began to rise and the way became more difficult. Still Wingenund did not slacken the pace. Nell, with a little help, managed to hold her own with Jim, but time after time the two of them had to wait for Mr. Wells to catch up. Once he got far behind, and Wingenund waited for them at the crest of a ridge, where the forest was open.

When they reached his side he stretched a long arm toward the sun, without speaking. They looked back.

Far in the west a great black and yellow cloud of smoke rolled skyward. It grew thinner as it soared aloft, until, high up, it lost its outline.

"Is it a forest fire?" Nell asked.

Jim did not voice his fear. He looked at Wingenund.

The Delaware stood silent a moment, still gazing westward, the dull glow of the setting sun reflected in his black eyes.

"Fire," he said. Then: "The sun sets tonight over the ashes of the Village of Peace."

Then he resumed his rapid march eastward. Saddened, the others followed him, Nell keeping close to Jim and the old man tramping after them with bowed head.

The sun set but Wingenund did not slacken his stride. Twilight deepened and still he kept on.

"Chief," Jim called at last, as Nell stumbled against him and Mr. Wells panted hoarsely behind them, "we can go no farther tonight. We must rest."

"Rest soon," Wingenund replied, and kept on.

Full dark had come when at last the Indian halted. They could see little, but they heard running water and felt soft moss under their feet.

They sank down wearily upon a large flat rock. Opening the pack, they found food and satisfied their hunger. Then they made themselves as comfortable as possible on the ground and fell asleep. Wingenund, alert and motionless, stood guard.

It seemed to Jim that he had just closed his eyes when he felt a gentle pressure on his arm.

"Day here," said the Indian.

Jim raised himself on his elbow and looked around. Nell was still asleep, the blanket tucked close up under her chin, the tumbled mass of her hair framing her pretty face.

"Nell, wake up," called Jim.

Her eyes opened wide. For a moment she stared, plainly not realizing where she was.

"Where—? Oh, I remember!" She sat up. "Oh, Jim, we're safe!—Aren't we?"

"Another day, and we'll be safe," he smiled.

She jumped up and shook out her rumpled skirt. "Let's fly!" she cried. "Come, Uncle!"

Mr. Wells lay quietly, his mild blue eyes smiling up at her, but he neither moved nor spoke.

"Eat, drink," said the Delaware, opening the pack.

"What a beautiful place!" the girl exclaimed, taking the bread and meat that was handed her. "Why, someone has camped here—see the screen of plaited ferns and the stone fireplace!"

"It seems to me this place looks familiar," Jim said, gazing around.

"Beautiful Spring," Wingenund informed them.

"Why, I know this place!" Nell cried. "I remember this glade, though I saw it before in moonlight. It was here that Wetzel rescued me from Girty!"

"Nell, you're right," Jim said. "Strange we should come here again!"

"Come, Uncle, you're lazy!" Nell said then, turning to Mr. Wells.

The old missionary lay still and smiled up at them.

"Uncle, you're not ill?" the girl cried.

"No, my dear, I'm not ill. But I'm done for—played out. I should never have tried to come with you. I'm too old for such mad hurrying. You must go along without me."

"Never!" Nell dropped to her knees beside him. "We shall wait here until you are rested enough to travel again."

"No," he said firmly. "It would not do for me to delay you when those—those beasts may be already on our trail. Leave me here. They would not hurt an old man."

"Mr. Wells, we'll wait—you'll be ready to travel in a short while," Jim protested.

"Jim, Nell—I have known all night that I could go no farther. It's all right, whatever happens to me. I am content. My work is finished. My only regret is that I brought you out to this wild frontier."

The girl bent over him, weeping. Jim sat down on

the other side and held his hand. For many moments no one spoke. Then the Delaware stood before them.

"Come," he said.

Nell pointed silently at her uncle.

"He is ill," said Jim to the Indian. "We can't leave him."

"We go," Wingenund said. "Leave old man. Leave food. Wingenund come back."

"The chief is right," said Mr. Wells. "You must go, for you are still in danger. I'll be all right until he gets back. Then we two can take our time."

Jim looked worriedly at Nell. The girl cried quietly.

Wingenund took most of the food that remained in the pack and left it by the old man.

"Come," he repeated.

"My Bible," said Mr. Wells, fumbling for the pocket where he always carried it.

Jim helped him get it out, and the old missionary opened it with fingers that trembled weakly.

"It will comfort me while I wait," he told them, and a smile lit up his thin face.

Nell bent and kissed him, then rose, her face pale and her lips pressed tight. Jim clasped his hand.

"Good-by, Nell—Jim," the old man murmured. "And God bless you, Wingenund. I shall wait here for you."

Turning away, the girl found the Delaware standing by her side. On an impulse she slid her hand into his large one, and looked up at him trustingly. The chief grasped her hand with a strong, warm pressure. She looked up at him, strangely thrilled. She knew that this savage warrior chief was her friend.

With a final wave of farewell, then, she and Jim started to leave the glade, following the tall Delaware. Then, suddenly, the chief stopped, with a low exclamation. They looked toward the opening into the woods where Wingenund's somber gaze was fixed.

Four painted savages stood there with rifles leveled. Behind them were Deering and Jim Girty.

Hope died in Jim's heart. The girl's lips parted to form a soundless cry of fear.

"Thought ye'd give me the slip, eh?" Girty jeered.

He strode forward to face Wingenund, his yellow eyes flashing. "Wal, chief, you've led me quite a chase."

Wingenund did not reply. He folded his arms, to stand silent and still.

The Indians then came into the glade and one of them quickly tied Jim's hands behind his back. They all wore a wild, brutish look, as if the fever to kill that had been aroused in them was not yet satisfied. One of them advanced menacingly toward Mr. Wells, where the old missionary still lay, watching the scene with horror in his eyes. But Wingenund said something to the man in Delaware and he stayed whatever action he had planned and slunk to one side of the glade.

"Jake," said Girty to his renegade friend, "come over here." He indicated the girl. "How d'ye like her?"

Nell stood before them, her face lowered and her hands clenched at her sides.

"She's a beauty," grinned Deering. "Purtiest gal I ever seed."

Girty scratched his whisker-stubbled chin with dirty fingers. Dark stains spotted the gaudy frills of his costume, his buckskin coat and leggings. His white eagle plumes, too, were spattered with dark spots.

"Ye may be interested to know I burned the Village o' Peace mainly to git you!" he said to her suddenly. "Come here to me—I got a big kiss fer ye."

He reached out an arm for her but she avoided his grasp. He jumped after her and seized her by her wrist.

"Here, now, don't come that on me," he growled. "Ye won't be so uppity, mebbe, arter you've been cookin' my meals and mendin' my clothes fer a few years! Come on, now—gimme that kiss—"

He pulled her toward him. Deering looked on with a grin. The Indians paced nervously about the glade. Jim lay on the moss, where he had been thrown, with closed eyes.

No one took notice of Wingenund. The chief stood back a little, screened by drooping branches.

His head turned a trifle to one side as he listened to some sound which his keen hearing had detected. Suddenly his gaze whipped to the gently quivering heads of some ferns on the far side of the clearing. Almost as he did so two sheets of flame burst from the ferns.

Spang! Spang!

Two rifle shots rang through the glade and two of Girty's Indians fell in their tracks.

Then a huge buckskin-clad body, spread out like a springing panther, hurtled upon Deering and Girty.

Nell reeled away as the two renegades went down, yelling. There began a terrific, whirling struggle.

Meanwhile, another figure in buckskin had charged the two remaining Indians, who were drawing their tomahawks. There came shrill cries, hoarse yells, and the sound of blows. One of the savages went down, twisted and writhed, and lay still. The other staggered, but fought on until a blow on his skull knocked him to his knees. He tried to rise, but another quick blow finished him.

The victor darted toward the wrestling men.

"Lew!" he shouted. "Shake him loose!" He swung his tomahawk high.

It was Jonathan Zane.

Baffled, he circled the knot of whirling wrestlers. Time and again he raised his weapon, only to lower it before he would risk a blow. Jim and Nell could hear the hoarse yells of Deering and the high-pitched, panic-stricken ones of Girty, but Wetzel himself seemed to utter no sound.

Suddenly Deering shot out from the struggling little group, as if from a catapult. He came down with a thud and Zane pounced upon him with cat-like quickness. The struggle that followed between him and the renegade was brief. The borderman stood up and Deering lay motionless.

Now Jonathan turned to Wetzel and Girty, not to aid his friend, but to watch the end which he knew must come.

Wetzel had risen to his feet and was clutching Girty with his left hand alone. His steel-like fingers were twisted in the renegade's shirt front near the throat so that Girty's breath was partly shut off. He was gasping noisily, his eyes bulging from his terror-stricken face.

Wetzel dragged him to a tree that stood by itself in the glade. He pushed him against it and held him there. Girty's hands pulled and tore at the powerful arm which forced him back against the tree trunk. It was no use. That arm was immovable.

Slowly the hunter raised his right arm. The blade in his hand, flashing in the light, pointed toward a near-by hilltop.

"Look thar, Girty," Wetzel said. "Thar's yer friends!"

On the dead branches of a tree on that hilltop sat

several great dark birds.

"*Buzzards!*" Wetzel hissed at him.

As Girty writhed and twisted in a desperate attempt to free himself, Jim divined the hunter's intent. It was too terrible a fate even for this scourge of the frontier, it seemed.

"No!" he cried out in protest. "Take him to Fort Henry—there he can be tried and executed."

"Downs," said Jonathan Zane, "this is the frontier. Jim Girty has killed some of our bravest friends in cold blood. This will be personal vengeance for Wetzel—but it will be justice too."

Then, as the hunter poised the knife, Jim Downs looked away.

CHAPTER TWENTY-SEVEN

TRAIL TEST

Jonathan Zane cut the young missionary's bonds. Jim ran to where the girl was kneeling, her head turned blindly against a tree to shut out the sight. Tenderly he lifted her to her feet, telling her that it was over. Zane bent over Mr. Wells, asking him if he was all right.

When he got to his feet it was to see the motionless figures of Wetzel and Wingenund facing each other. The chief stood erect, his arms folded, his face calm. Wetzel was slightly crouched, his eyes burning, his lips twitching.

"Now look here, Lew," said Zane, stepping toward him.

If Wetzel heard him he gave no sign. Then, with a single flashing motion he had his tomahawk in one hand and started toward the chief.

"Lew, wait a minute!" roared Jonathan.

"Wetzel, wait, wait!" cried Jim, leaping to grasp the hunter by the arm. He was flung aside.

"No, Wetzel—for heaven's sake, no!" the girl screamed.

She threw herself in front of him. Frantically she

grasped his hands and looked up into his frenzied face.

The hunter halted. "Let go, girl!" he said hoarsely.

"No, no!" she repeated. "You must not touch him, Wetzel—he is a friend!"

"Wingenund is my enemy," he said.

"Listen," she pleaded. "Wingenund helped us get away. He warned me to flee from Girty. He was guiding us to Fort Henry. He did his best to save me —all of us. For my sake, Wetzel, do not hurt him— do not spill any more blood. Why, Wingenund is a Christian!"

Wetzel stepped back, breathing heavily.

"Would you kill a Christian?" the girl said, pressing her advantage.

"I reckon not, but this Injun ain't a Christian," the hunter said slowly.

"Put away your weapon," she urged him. "Forget your enmity. You must be merciful—brave men are always merciful."

"Injun," Wetzel shot at the Delaware, "are you a Christian?"

Wingenund made no reply. He did not move.

"Oh, tell him you are a Christian!" the girl appealed to Wingenund.

"Yellow-hair," he said with dignity, "Wingenund is true to his race."

"Injun," Wetzel said menacingly, stepping toward

him again, "my back bears the scars of your warriors' whips."

"Deathwind's scars are deep, but the Delaware's are deeper," came the reply. "Wingenund's heart bears two scars. His son lies under the moss and ferns. Deathwind killed him. Wingenund's daughter freed the Delaware's great foe, and betrayed her father. Can the Christian God tell Wingenund of his child?"

"Delaware, your daughter is on the way to Fort Henry with her husband and Yellow-hair's sister," Wetzel said, looking into the chief's eyes.

Nell uttered a glad cry, for this was her first knowledge that Kate had been rescued. Jim, too, smiled in relief, in spite of the tense situation, and Mr. Wells broke down and cried.

"Delaware, we are sworn foes," Wetzel said challengingly to the Indian.

"Wingenund asks no mercy."

"Are you a Christian?" the hunter demanded again.

"Wingenund is true to his race."

"Delaware, go!" Wetzel snapped. "Take these weapons and go. When your shadow falls shortest on the ground, Deathwind starts on your trail."

"If Deathwind thirsts for Wingenund's blood, let him spill it now, for when the Delaware goes into the forest his trail will fade."

"Go!" roared Wetzel, his eyes ablaze.

Silently Wingenund picked up some of the weapons of the dead Indians and stalked from the glade.

"Come," said Jonathan to the others. "We must start out for Fort Henry. We can rig a litter for Mr. Wells, Downs. You and I can carry him."

An hour later the four left the glade. As Jim and Nell left they looked back once. The bodies of Deering and the Indians lay where they had fallen. The tall figure of Wetzel stood in silence, watching his shadow. Their eyes avoided glancing toward the tree to which a gaudily dressed figure was impaled with a long hunting knife.

The fleeting humane impulse which had prompted Wetzel to give Wingenund a chance for his life now gave way to the habit of years. Once again he was the ruthless hunter of Indians.

A fierce, tingling joy surged through him as he struck the Delaware's trail. Wingenund had made little or no effort to hide his tracks. He had gone northwest, straight as the crow flies, toward the Indian encampment.

The hunter's method of trailing an Indian was unusual. He did not rely only on sight, on finding sign. Often he would guess his victim's intentions. He did not always stick to the Indian's tracks.

For half a mile he followed closely the Delaware's plainly marked trail. Then he stopped to take a quick survey of the forest before him. Abruptly he

"Go!" Wetzel Roared, His Eyes Ablaze

left the trail and, breaking into a run, he went for a quarter of a mile, then stopped to listen. All seemed well.

He lowered his head and walked along slowly, examining the moss and leaves. Presently he came to a little open space where the soil was sandy.

He bent over, then rose quickly. He had come upon the Delaware's trail. Cautiously he moved forward, stopping every minute to listen.

The trail led to a rocky ridge and there disappeared. He made no effort to find the chief's footprints on the flinty ground, but halted a moment and studied the ridge and the lay of the land—a ravine on one side and a dark, impassable forest on the other.

Then, satisfied that he had guessed the Delaware's intention, he slipped down the bank of the ravine and leaped lightly from stone to stone, over fallen logs and the brawling brook. At every turn of the ravine and at every open place he stopped to listen.

Arriving at the head of the ravine, he left it and crossed some rising ground. He listened to the birds and searched the grass and leaves. He found not the slightest trace of any trail. He retraced his steps, carefully studying every inch of the ground. But it was all in vain. Wingenund had begun to show his savage cunning.

Still calm and patient, Wetzel took a minute to think back. The Delaware had not crossed the ridge, then. He had simply been cunning enough to make his pursuer think that he intended to.

The hunter hurried to the eastern end of the ridge, solely because that was the course the Delaware seemed to have the least reason to take. He was drawing near to the end of the ridge when his questing eyes caught sight of something that caused him to drop to his knees.

It was a twisted bit of fern, with the drops of dew brushed off. Wetzel examined the grass around it. He was convinced that he had located the trail, but he was still ignorant of its direction.

Slowly he traced twisted ferns and bruised leaves down over the side of the ridge and, at last, near a stone, he found a moccasin print in the moss. It pointed east. The Delaware had almost completely reversed his former direction. Moreover, he was showing extreme cunning in hiding his trail.

No more did Wetzel trust to guesswork. He realized that his own woodcraft was matched. Now he stuck close to the trail, as does a hungry wolf to that of his quarry.

It led over logs, stones, and hard-baked ground. It led up stony ravines and over cliffs. The wily chief was using all of his skill. He walked backward over moss and sand where his footprints showed plainly. He leaped wide openings in the rock, then jumped back again. He let himself down over ledges by branches. He crossed creeks and gorges by swinging himself into trees and climbing from one to another. He waded hard-bottomed brooks and avoided swampy, soft ground.

Doggedly Wetzel stuck to the gradually fading trail. As time went by he was forced to go more and more slowly in order to find any sign of the Delaware's passing. The only thing that was clear was that Wingenund was slowly swinging to the southwest, a course that took him farther and farther away from the Delaware camp.

Slowly it dawned upon the hunter that Wingenund could hardly have any reason for taking this circling course other than one of pride and a kind of joy in misleading his trailer, in fooling the foe of the Delawares, in showing Deathwind that there was one Indian who could laugh at him and lose him in the forest.

To be led on a wild-goose chase! This was indeed a bitter pill for Wetzel to swallow. Fury swept through him. Earnestly his dark eyes searched the ground.

Yet in spite of his anger he felt some new sensation creeping over him. He remembered that Wingenund had offered his life.

Slowly Wetzel passed up and down the ridges, through the forest aisles, across the little flowing brooks, out upon the open fields—always close on the trail.

Then, in an open part of the forest, where a fire

had once swept away the brush and the smaller trees, he came upon the spot where the trail ended.

There in the soft ground was a moccasin print. The trees were not thick, so there was plenty of light. Presently Wetzel discovered another moccasin print.

Yet that was all. Over all that glade no further evidence of the Delaware's trail could he find.

Wetzel searched every square inch of the ground round about, crawling on his hands and knees. Again and again he went over it. The fact that one of the clearly visible prints pointed west and the other one east was the most baffling thing that he had ever experienced in all his wanderings.

At last he admitted to himself that he had failed. Somehow the Delaware fox had outwitted him. He took the defeat hard, for he had grown accustomed to thinking of himself as unfailing on the trail.

With head bowed, he made his way westward, his steps slow and dragging. The land was strange to him, but he was sure that he was going toward familiar ground. He walked slowly and quietly, his rage at Wingenund and at himself slowly subsiding.

On the summit of a high ridge he looked around to get his bearings. He was surprised to find that he had apparently traveled in a great circle. Below him rose the tall oak tree which was the landmark of Beautiful Spring.

He went toward the spring, with the idea in mind that he had not scalped the Indians who had fallen in the fight that morning. He crossed a stretch of open meadow, heading for the grove that surrounded the spring.

Suddenly he halted. Something seemed out of harmony in the numberless little sounds of the forest. He sank into the tall weeds and listened. Then he crawled a little farther.

A single note of an oriole warned him. After that he scarcely needed the quick notes of a catbird to tell him that near at hand, somewhere, was another human being.

The hot blood leaped through his veins. But calmly, coldly, silently, he began his familiar crawling stalk of his game.

On he went, under briars and thickets, across hollows full of yellow leaves, over stony patches of ground. At last he reached the fern-covered knoll which overlooked the glade. To its crest he glided, lithe and sinuous, his movements as tigerish as his heart.

He parted the long ferns. Eyes glistening, he gazed down into the glade.

There was Wingenund, squatting before the flames of a small, smokeless fire. He was slowly turning a green stick which held a strip of meat. He seemed unheeding of the possibility of being found.

Wetzel sank back into the ferns. A savage, unreasoning joy gripped him, and he must still it before he did anything.

Breathing hard, he lay there, gripping his rifle tightly. Slowly he mastered the passion that might spoil his aim.

The Delaware's life was his to take at last, and he swore he would have it. He trembled violently, then with a mighty effort calmed himself. He eased forward and raised his long-barreled rifle.

He stared. Wingenund now stood erect. Arms folded, he was facing in Wetzel's direction, and his eyes seemed to be fixed directly on the clump of ferns behind which the hunter crouched.

Suddenly he spread his arms wide, low at his sides, and the proud chin tilted challengingly.

The gesture was unmistakable. Wingenund knew he was there, and again was offering the hunter the chance to take his life.

Suddenly Wetzel grinned to himself. *The old fox!* he thought. *He knows he shook me off his trail, and now he knows, somehow, that I only found him by accident. So he figgers he can die happy.* The rifle barrel lowered. *Well, I ain't goin' to give him the satisfaction!*

Laying the gun down, Wetzel stepped out from cover. Wingenund looked at him without speaking.

The hunter approached and when he was near the Delaware turned to the fire, picked up the strip of meat on the stick, and held it out to the white man.

Wetzel hesitated but a moment before he took the meat. Wingenund grunted in approval, speared another strip with the stick, and began to cook it.

Neither spoke until hunger had been satisfied. Then Wetzel said:

"You won, chief. Deathwind lost the trail."

"Nobody follow Wingenund's trail." It was not boasting, but a mere statement of fact.

"Tell me with a straight tongue now, chief," Wetzel said after a silence, "are you a Christian?"

The Delaware looked the hunter in the eye.

"Wingenund is a Christian," he said. Then: "Wingenund could not say he was a Christian to save his life."

Wetzel nodded. He understood.

CHAPTER TWENTY-EIGHT

WETZEL ANSWERS A QUESTION

It was late afternoon at Fort Henry. The red sun had already sunk behind the wooded hill, and the long shadows of the trees lengthened on the green square in front of the fort.

Colonel Zane stood in his doorway watching the river with eager eyes. A few minutes before, a man had appeared on the bank of the island and hailed. The colonel had sent Jonathan to find out what was wanted. His brother had already reached the island in his flatboat, and soon the little craft was putting back out with the stranger seated at the stern.

I thought it might be Wetzel, mused the colonel, *but then I never knew Lew to use the boat.*

Jonathan brought the man across the river and up the winding path to where Colonel Zane waited.

"Hello! It's young Christy!" exclaimed the colonel, jumping off the steps and extending his hand to the youthful preacher whom Jim had met with Captain Williamson's party.

"Glad to see you!" the colonel boomed. "Where's Williamson—and how did you happen over here?"

"Captain Williamson and his men will make the river eight or ten miles above here," answered Christy. "I came across to inquire about the people who left the Village of Peace with Wingenund. Jonathan tells me they got out all right."

"Indeed they did—all of them, thank heaven. Come in and sit down," the colonel invited. "You'll stay overnight, of course."

"Thank you, I will," Christy responded. "I'm feeling pretty tired."

"No wonder, after going through that bad business at the mission. You'll have to tell us about it. Sam Brady came through yesterday, and spoke of seeing you over there. Well, here's Jim now!"

The young missionary came through the door and he and the newcomer shook hands warmly.

"How is the young lady?" asked Christy, when the first greetings were over.

"Nell is beginning to get over the shock. She'll be glad to see you, I know."

"Jonathan tells me that Mr. Wells united you two in marriage day before yesterday."

"Yes," Jim smiled. "We had intended to wait awhile, but Nell's uncle was afraid he wasn't going to live and since he wanted to perform the ceremony himself we consented to hurry the wedding a bit. Of course, he was unduly worried about his health. He was simply exhausted by the tragedy and then the long trip, and he's already gaining back his strength."

"I'm glad to hear it—both of your marriage and that Mr. Wells is on the mend."

"You look thin and haggard yourself."

"That awful time pulled me down. I was an unwilling onlooker at the whole horrible business, and I fear I shall never get over it. I can still see those painted devils, running around with the fresh scalps of their own people. I actually counted the bodies of seventy-six Christian Indians afterward. An hour after you left, the church was in ashes. Jim Girty was in the forefront of everything—the worst savage of them all."

"Did you hear of his death?" Colonel Zane asked quietly.

"Yes, and a fitting end it was," Christy said grimly. "Has Wetzel been in since?"

"No. Jonathan says he went after Wingenund, so there's no telling when he'll return."

"I hoped he would spare the Delaware."

"Wetzel spare an Indian?" The colonel smiled at the thought.

"But the chief certainly acted as a friend—he saved the girl at the village."

"Yes, I know, and I don't feel right about it. Wingenund is a good Indian, but Wetzel seems to be unmoved by such things."

"Here's Nell," Jim announced proudly, "and Mrs. Clarke, too."

Nell appeared in the doorway with Colonel Zane's

sister. The two of them greeted the young man.

"I'm so glad you got away safely from—from there," Christy said earnestly to Nell.

"Tell me about Benny," the girl begged.

"Benny?—Oh, yes, the little Indian boy! He is safe and well. Heckewelder kept him hidden until it was all over. As soon as it's possible he's going to get the boy away from there. He'll see that he gets an education."

"Oh, I am so glad," Nell breathed in relief.

"And the missionaries?" inquired Jim.

"They were all well when I left. Edwards has entirely recovered, and even Young is well on the road to recovery, although it will be many weeks before he's himself again."

"Thank heaven!" said Jim. "You remember I told you of Nell's sister, Kate, and how she'd been kidnaped. She's here now, gradually coming back to normal—she is engaged to marry Young, you know."

"And your brother?"

"Here, too. He suffered some bad wounds, but he is strong as a bear and is practically well already. I expect he'll be with us shortly— What do the missionaries plan to do?"

"They say they will stay out there and try to make a new start, but I'm afraid it's impossible."

"It *is* impossible," Colonel Zane asserted. "Not so much because the Indian doesn't want Christianity, but on account of Girty's rule. The Village of Peace was really ruined by the renegades."

"Captain Williamson could have prevented the massacre," Jim declared.

"Well, possibly," the colonel responded. "It was a hard decision for him to make. Still, I think he was wrong not to try."

"Hullo!" cried Jonathan Zane. He rose from the steps, where he had been sitting and listening to the conversation.

A soft-moccasined footfall sounded on the path. They all turned to see Wetzel coming slowly toward them. His buckskin hunting-suit was ragged and worn. He looked tired, but his dark eyes were calm.

They greeted him warmly. Nell gave him both her hands and smiled up at him.

"I'm so glad you're home safe," she said.

"Safe and sound, lass," he replied, "and glad to find you well. Did Joe and the Injun gal and your sister git here all right?"

She nodded emphatically and his infrequent smile lighted up his face.

He leaned on his long rifle, looking from Nell to the colonel's sister.

"Betty," he said to the latter, "I've allus give you fust place among border gals, but here's one as could run you a real race," he said earnestly.

"Why, Lew Wetzel making compliments!" exclaimed the colonel's sister. "Of all things!"

Jonathan Zane stood silently, studying Wetzel's

face closely. The colonel observed him doing this, and guessing the cause, said:

"Tell us, Lew, did you find Wingenund?"

"Yes," he answered simply.

"Did you get him over the sight of your rifle?" the colonel pressed.

The hunter nodded.

A chill crept over the others. Nell bowed her head and stifled a sob. Jim turned away, biting his lip. Christy looked out across the valley. Colonel Zane picked up a pebble and tossed it idly from one hand to the other. Jonathan continued to stare at Wetzel.

The colonel's sister fixed her great black eyes on Wetzel's face.

"Well, Lew?" she asked quietly.

The hunter was silent for a long moment. Then he met her eyes directly and the shadow of a smile seemed to touch his lips.

"Betty," he said, "I missed him."

Then, shouldering his long rifle, he strode away.

WHITMAN BOOKS
FOR BOYS AND GIRLS

NEW STORIES
OF ADVENTURE AND MYSTERY

Up-to-the-minute novels for boys and girls about favorite characters, all popular and well known—

ROY ROGERS and the Outlaws of Sundown Valley
ROY ROGERS and the Ghost of Mystery Rancho
ROY ROGERS and the Gopher Creek Gunman
ROY ROGERS and the Raiders of Sawtooth Ridge

GENE AUTRY and the Badmen of Broken Bow
GENE AUTRY and the Golden Ladder Gang
GENE AUTRY and the Thief River Outlaws
GENE AUTRY and the Redwood Pirates

ZANE GREY'S The Spirit of the Border
ZANE GREY'S The Last Trail

RED RYDER and the Riddle of Roaring Range
RED RYDER and the Adventure at Chimney Rock
RED RYDER and the Secret of the Lucky Mine

BLONDIE and DAGWOOD'S Adventure in Magic
BLONDIE and DAGWOOD'S Marvelous Invention

WHITMAN BOOKS
FOR BOYS AND GIRLS

NEW STORIES
OF ADVENTURE AND MYSTERY

THE BOBBSEY TWINS: Merry Days Indoors and Out
THE BOBBSEY TWINS in the Country
THE BOBBSEY TWINS at the Seashore

THE WALTON BOYS in High Country
THE WALTON BOYS in Rapids Ahead
THE WALTON BOYS and Gold in the Snow

TOM STETSON and the Blue Devil
TOM STETSON and the Giant Jungle Ants
TOM STETSON on the Trail of the Lost Tribe

A BOY SAILOR with John Paul Jones
A BOY FIGHTER with Andrew Jackson

GINNY GORDON and the Mystery at the Old Barn
GINNY GORDON and the Mystery of the Missing Heirloom
GINNY GORDON and the Disappearing Candlesticks

TRIXIE BELDEN and the Gatehouse Mystery
TRIXIE BELDEN and the Red Trailer Mystery
TRIXIE BELDEN and the Secret of the Mansion